CLASSIFIED

To: Agent Zachary Steele

From: U.S. Customs Officials

Subject: Chloe Betancourt

Congratulations, Agent Steele. Your sterling performance in the field—and your typing ability—make you the best-qualified agent for the Betancourt case. The objective is to gain information on prime subject Chloe Betancourt…as her personal secretary. Therefore, phone, file, fetch, do whatever you have to do to keep things authentic—but get the bugs in place and earn her trust. So far, we have no solid evidence against the subject. Use your undercover talents to get close…and get the proof we need. The subject is quite beautiful, but I'm sure you need no reminder to keep your personal feelings separate from the job.

Be careful out there, Agent.

And Merry Christmas!

CLASSIFIED

Dear Reader,

Christmas is here once again. It seems hard to believe it's been twelve months since the last time, but it has. And once again our present to you is made up of two wonderful Christmas romances from two of our most popular Yours Truly authors.

In *A Husband for Christmas*, Jo Ann Algermissen comes up with a terrific premise to create a boss/secretary romance that will have you laughing out loud. The boss/secretary pairing is a classic one, of course, but she really brings it into the '90s in this ultra-enjoyable romp. Then take a look at *Secret Agent Santa*, by Linda Lewis. It's that boss/secretary thing again—but with another unpredictable twist. Picture a tough undercover agent having to pose as a secretary to a Southern belle. Sparks are sure to fly—especially 'cuz this is one Santa you'll long to kiss under the mistletoe.

And so another year draws to a close. But don't worry. Because we'll be back next year—all year!—with more of the fun and flirtatious tales of romance you've come to expect from Silhouette Yours Truly, the line all about unexpectedly meeting—and marrying!—Mr. Right.

Happy Holidaze!

Leslie Wainger
Executive Senior Editor

Please address questions and book requests to:
Silhouette Reader Service
U.S.: 3010 Walden Ave., P.O. Box 1325, Buffalo, NY 14269
Canadian: P.O. Box 609, Fort Erie, Ont. L2A 5X3

LINDA LEWIS

Secret Agent Santa

OFFICIALLY WITHDRAWN FROM
PIONEERLAND LIBRARY SYSTEM

Pioneerland Library System
P.O. Box 327
410 5th St. SW
Willmar, MN 56201

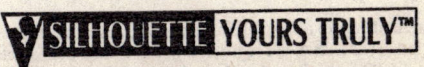

Published by Silhouette Books
America's Publisher of Contemporary Romance

If you purchased this book without a cover you should be aware that this book is stolen property. It was reported as "unsold and destroyed" to the publisher, and neither the author nor the publisher has received any payment for this "stripped book."

This book is dedicated to my two favorite
MJs: my sister, Mary Jane,
and my editor, Melissa Jeglinski

SILHOUETTE BOOKS

ISBN 0-373-52082-4

SECRET AGENT SANTA

Copyright © 1998 by Linda Kay West

All rights reserved. Except for use in any review, the reproduction or utilization of this work in whole or in part in any form by any electronic, mechanical or other means, now known or hereafter invented, including xerography, photocopying and recording, or in any information storage or retrieval system, is forbidden without the written permission of the editorial office, Silhouette Books, 300 East 42nd Street, New York, NY 10017 U.S.A.

All characters in this book have no existence outside the imagination of the author and have no relation whatsoever to anyone bearing the same name or names. They are not even distantly inspired by any individual known or unknown to the author, and all incidents are pure invention.

This edition published by arrangement with Harlequin Books S.A.

® and TM are trademarks of Harlequin Books S.A., used under license. Trademarks indicated with ® are registered in the United States Patent and Trademark Office, the Canadian Trade Marks Office and in other countries.

Printed in U.S.A.

Dear Reader,

Writing about Chloe's Christmas tree reminded me of the year we almost didn't have a tree. My sister and I thought we wouldn't be able to make it home for Christmas, but at the last minute our plans changed and we headed for home. When we arrived late on Christmas Eve, there was *no* Christmas tree. Our father hadn't gotten one, since he thought he'd be spending Christmas alone. We went searching for a tree. We looked everywhere, but all the Christmas-tree lots were closed and bare. Dismayed, but not defeated, we went to a grocery store—also closed—that had sold trees. We drove around the back of the store, and there it was. One leftover Christmas tree, tossed in a Dumpster. We rescued it, took it home and decorated it. Like Chloe and Zach, I've had my share of perfect trees, but the one I'll never forget is the scraggly tree we found in the trash.

Linda Lewis

Books by Linda Lewis

Silhouette Yours Truly

Cinderella and the Texas Prince
Secret Agent Santa

Silhouette Romance

Honeymoon Suite #1113
The Husband Hunt #1135
Cowboy Seeks Perfect Wife #1226

Prologue

Trying not to pant, Zachary Steele entered the office on the second floor of the United States Custom House in New Orleans. Maybe he shouldn't have taken the marble stairs two at a time. He would have taken it slow and easy if the guard, an attractive female, hadn't given him that pitying look. Zach hated being pitied, almost as much as he hated being weak and out of shape.

He stopped in front of the secretary's desk. "I'm Zachary Steele. Has the pre-op meeting started?"

The woman glanced pointedly at the clock on the wall. "I doubt it. They're waiting for you in the conference room." In case he hadn't gotten the message, she added, "You're late."

"I know. Where is the meeting?"

"Go back to the hallway, take a right, two doors down."

Zach followed the directions to the conference room and walked in without knocking. Three men and a woman were seated at an oval table. He recognized the S.A.C. and one of the other agents seated at the table, but not the third man, and not the woman.

"About time you showed up, Steele," said John Allen, the Special Agent in Charge. "Gentlemen, this is our undercover agent, Zachary Steele. He's just been released from rehab. Things got a little dicey on his last assignment, and Zach took a couple of bullets.

"Zach, you know Jeremy Baker. Bobby Williams is the case agent in charge of this investigation. Marilyn Charles is the tech agent. Once you're in place, she'll wire the premises for sound and pictures. Baker will be your contact."

The agents stood and shook hands with Zach.

"Okay, Bobby, let's start the meeting."

"This investigation started with a request from our counterparts in Colombia," Bobby began. "They've traced stolen pre-Columbian artifacts to coffee shipments to the United States and asked for our help following the trail on this end. We have conclusive proof that the shipments ended up at Betancourt Coffees, right here in New Orleans. We've had the owner's telephone tapped for several weeks, but nothing incriminating has turned up. That's why we asked for an undercover operation. We need someone on-site, to monitor the shipments and to find out where and how the goods are being distributed. We got the approval for the undercover last week, and reportedly Steele is the best-qualified U.C.A. for this job." The case agent eyed Steele, doubt written clearly on his face.

"I have worked art smuggling cases before," Zach said mildly. "And I'm in better shape than I look." Marginally better, according to the doctor who'd examined him that morning. His medical records had been transferred from Washington to New Orleans along with only tentative approval for Zach to return to active duty. He'd been forced to plead with the doctor to remove "tentative" from the report.

Zach hated having to beg.

"You've got a week or so before you go on-site. And this job shouldn't get physical, anyway," said the case agent. He sounded as if he was reassuring himself, not Zach. "All we need from you is close surveillance of the target."

"I can handle that. And I know a little about pre-Columbian artifacts."

"We know," said John. "You wrote the training manual on the subject. But that's not the main reason we wanted you for this job."

"No? What else?"

"You can type."

1

"I need a man." Chloe Betancourt wrinkled her nose in disgust. "I *hate* needing a man."

"I know you do," Sylvie Sheridan murmured sympathetically as she strolled around Chloe's office, straightening pictures and rearranging knickknacks. "Too bad about Mark."

"How could he do that? He just up and got married. One minute he was my Mr. Dependable, the man I could always count on to take me places, and the next minute he's some stranger's husband." Chloe exaggerated a little—Mark had stopped being available for several months before his marriage. She hadn't fully realized her loss until the holiday season arrived with all its business-masquerading-as-social events.

"You should have married him."

"That was never an option. Mark and I were friends, not lovers."

"Well, then. You can't blame him for moving on to someone else."

"But he moved so *fast*," complained Chloe.

"I heard his bride wanted a fall wedding," said

Sylvie, straightening the calendar on the wall opposite Chloe's desk.

The calendar open on her desk momentarily distracted Chloe. She'd circled Saturday, the twenty-eighth of November, in red to mark the date the next shipment would arrive from the Finca Velásquez, the coffee estate in Colombia that now supplied the bulk of Betancourt Coffees's raw product. She had to be ready—

"Chloe?" Sylvie waved a hand in front of Chloe's face. "Are you with me?"

"Yes. Sorry. What were you saying?"

"Mark's bride wanted an autumn wedding. That's why things happened so fast." Sylvie perched on the edge of Chloe's oversize desk, greedily rubbing her hand over the smooth surface. "That way they'll be back from their honeymoon before Christmas."

Sylvie coveted the antique mahogany monster, Chloe knew, and her friend had offered to buy it on more than one occasion. Chloe had no plans to sell it, however. The desk was one of the few things her father had left her that had not caused her grief. "I know," Chloe said glumly. "Mark's family has a big open house every Christmas Eve. I've already received an invitation, for me and a 'guest.' But who could that be? I don't know anyone I'd be willing to ask."

Sylvie shrugged. "You could go alone."

"I've tried that." Chloe gave a delicate shudder. "It was horrible. All those men, panting and pawing. Why do they behave that way?"

"I don't know, Chloe. Could it be they find curvaceous little blondes with big blue eyes cute?" Sylvie curved her lips in a feline smile.

"So they say." Glancing in the mirror on the wall opposite her desk, Chloe shrugged. She would have preferred being described as attractive rather than cute, but she didn't have the height for it. For years she'd tried to add inches every way she could think of, from impossibly high heels to big hair. The heels had hurt her feet and the big hair had made her look top-heavy. So she'd accepted being short. Now her leather pumps had a sensible two-inch heel, and her blond hair curved around her cheekbones in a short bob.

Still looking at herself in the mirror, Chloe acknowledged that she had good cheekbones. And a nice, straight nose to go with them. Her mouth was all right, too, although she wouldn't mind having lips just a little bit fuller. Grinning boldly, Chloe answered Sylvie's tongue-in-cheek question. "Personally, I think Betancourt Coffees's bottom line is more of a lure than I am. At least I knew Mark cared about me, not my company."

"Mark Michelet is one of the richest men in town. You never should have let him go."

"He was never mine to let go. Once Mark decided he wanted a wife, I was out of the picture. He knows how I feel about marriage. I will never give a man that kind of control over me."

"Maybe you could have compromised on some

sort of marriage of convenience. Mark didn't seem like the domineering kind to me."

"He wasn't—while we were dating. That doesn't mean anything. It's only after they have their ring on your finger and their name tacked on to yours that they change into...know-it-all, dictatorial *beasts*."

"You can't judge all men by your father, Chloe."

"Oh, yes, I can."

"I promise, there are a few good men around."

"Maybe. I don't have time to look for one." Chloe's gaze returned to the calendar on the opposite wall. Propping her chin on her laced fingers, she said, "If I did have time, I know just what I'd want. A man who was agreeable and soft-spoken. And convenient. He ought to live down the street and be available whenever I need him."

Sylvie raised an eyebrow. "Really? I thought most of your so-called social events were really business. But that sounds more...personal. Tell me again. What, exactly, do you need a man for?"

Chloe drummed her fingers on the edge of the desk. "Not *that*. I can do without that."

"I'm sure you can. But why would you?"

Chloe dismissed Sylvie's question with a wave of her hand. "Sex is one more thing men use to control women. All I want is a man to take me to a dinner or a cocktail party. Or a ball." Chloe shot her friend a horrified look. "Sylvie, holiday season is here."

"Isn't that what I just said?"

"I would have to live in the only city where holiday season lasts from Thanksgiving to Mardi Gras." Chloe buried her head in her hands.

"Some people start at Halloween and end at Jazz Fest," murmured Sylvie.

Raising her head, Chloe moaned, "There will be Christmas parties, New Year's parties, Mardi Gras balls. I'll have to attend at least some of them."

"Yes, you will." Sylvie nodded, her dark eyes sparkling mischievously. "Tell me more about your dream man."

"He's not a dream, he's an impossibility. I'll never find a man who would be there when I needed him as an escort, but who would go away and leave me alone once I finished with him. No male is going to be that cooperative." Leaning back in her oversize leather chair, Chloe sighed. "Too bad. I'd pay big bucks for a man like that."

Sylvie gazed thoughtfully at Chloe. "You do realize you're describing what used to be called a gigolo."

"Am I?" She chewed on that thought for a second. *Gigolo* conjured up an image of a man with slicked-back hair, a smooth line and an expensive price tag. Not quite what she'd had in mind, although a modern version—if such an animal existed—might have his uses. "I have a feeling that gigolos, like good men, are in short supply."

"You might be surprised. I'll admit I've never seen a Gigolos 'R' Us, but you could advertise."

"I don't think so."

"Sure you could—one of those personal ads." Sylvie closed her eyes. "I can see it now. 'Wanted. Gigolo. Handsome, convenient man to provide escort services on demand to attractive woman. Generous salary, health insurance. Other benefits negotiable.'"

"Sylvie Sheridan! You're a wicked woman. That would be tacky beyond belief."

Raising her shoulder in a negligent shrug, Sylvie said, "If you don't want to advertise, you can always ask Santa to bring you your very own gigolo."

A discreet knock sounded on the door.

"Come in," said Chloe.

A man bearing a tray with a silver coffee service and two cups entered the office. "Your coffee, Ms. Betancourt."

"Thank you, Zachary. Sylvie, you haven't met my new assistant, have you? Zachary, this is Sylvie Sheridan. She owns the Sheridan Gallery on Julia Street. Sylvie, Zachary Steele. He's taking Marie's place while she's on maternity leave."

"Ms. Sheridan. How do you take your coffee?"

After a long pause, during which Sylvie gave the man a thorough once-over, she said, "Cream and sugar. I'm from New York, you see. As Chloe has pointed out to me on many occasions, East Coast folks are wimps when it comes to coffee. It takes a woman raised on dark roast to drink this stuff black."

"Stuff? You're calling my personal blend 'stuff'?" Chloe demanded with mock indignation. "I can't believe that after almost twenty years in New Orleans, you still prefer that dishwater that passes for coffee in the East."

"Sorry." With a rueful smile, Sylvie turned her attention back to Chloe. "Tell me more about this evening. What particular social function put you in need of an escort?"

"A reception honoring Gerald Cox."

"Who is he?"

"He owns a chain of coffeehouses on the East Coast—Cox's Coffee Emporiums. He's already expanded to Florida, and he's thinking of bringing them to the rest of the Gulf Coast."

"And you want to make sure he knows how New Orleanians like their coffee."

Chloe gave an emphatic nod. "Dark and rich and with the Betancourt label. But if I go to the reception alone, I'll spend most of the evening avoiding those—"

"Lascivious Lotharios?"

"Men. And Emile Arcenaux will monopolize Mr. Cox."

"Ah, yes, Emile. Your nemesis. How is the C.E.O. of Creole Coffees?"

"Doing well, unfortunately. Not that I wish him ill. All I want is a level playing field. I swear that man sics his cousins on me just to keep me from networking."

"But if you had a date, he could run interference for you and give you time to charm Mr. Cox."

"Exactly." Chloe smiled at Zachary as he filled a china cup with black coffee and handed it to her.

"I wish I knew someone, but my little black book is sadly lacking in the kind of man you need." Sylvie took a sip of coffee, her gaze following Zachary as he left the office. "What's wrong with him?"

"The limp? I'm not sure. He only started a couple of weeks ago, and I've been out of the office a lot since he started. The office was closed yesterday. Thanksgiving, you know. Maybe I should have closed the office today, too, but I had a sales meeting and so...here we are."

Chloe heard herself babble, but she couldn't seem to stop. At least she hadn't confessed that she'd stayed away from the office on purpose. She had needed time to come to terms with her initial reaction to Zachary Steele. She had *liked* the idea of being his boss, of having him available and willing to obey her every command. What on earth could that mean?

She had always thought of herself as an enlightened employer, a woman who wouldn't discriminate, intimidate or intentionally irritate an employee for any reason, certainly not on the basis of sex. She made the coffee as often as Marie did, for one thing. And she'd had other men working for her for years.

But never in the next office. And never a man so eager to do anything she asked of her. It gave her a heady sense of power, as well as the uneasy feeling that it was a kind of power that could be abused. "I think he may have been in some kind of accident. His résumé showed that he'd been unemployed for several months, and the woman at Temps said he'd been in the hospital during that time."

"No, I mean why can't *he* take you to the party? He's a bit scrawny, but otherwise...not bad-looking.

I've always liked them tall, dark and wounded. His eyes are the same color as coffee beans, did you notice?"

"My assistant?" Chloe's gaze strayed to the door leading to the outer office. "Coffee-colored eyes? I suppose so, if you mean dark roast, not medium." Unreadable, either way. Rarely could she tell what he was thinking. A few times, though, she'd looked up and seen something in his gaze that seemed to mirror her guilty fantasies. She was almost sure Zachary wanted her.

"Where did you find him, anyway?" Sylvie asked.

"At Temps Unlimited, the same place I always use for Marie's replacement when she's on maternity leave."

"How many does this make for her?"

"Three. All boys. Marie swears she's not going to stop until she has a girl."

Sylvie tilted her head to one side. "Interesting that you chose a male secretary."

Chloe frowned. "I didn't have a choice. He was the only one available." That had been unusual. The two previous times she'd asked for a replacement for Marie, she'd had several résumés to choose from. The agency had explained that the lack of applicants resulted from the low unemployment rate in Southern Louisiana."

"You could have gone to another agency."

"I suppose so. But Zachary more than met all the qualifications for the position. He types ninety words a minute, and he knows our word-processing and accounting software. I couldn't have asked for a more efficient, willing assistant."

"One wonders why a man like that would be satisfied with clerical work."

"I asked him about that during the interview. Before this job, he worked in various retail establishments, usually in management, sometimes in sales. He said since he'd been off for a while, he wanted to ease back into the workforce in a less stressful job. That's why he signed up with the Temps agency."

"That makes sense, I suppose. Well, if he's your assistant, why don't you ask him to assist you this evening?"

"I couldn't do that," Chloe insisted, trying to ignore the tingling sensation slithering up her spine. She had asked men out on occasion, before she and Mark had become a predictable twosome. She didn't remember that doing so could be so...stimulating. "It's not in his job description."

"Not in Marie's, you mean. You're the boss. You can rewrite the job description."

"That wouldn't be fair." He might think he couldn't refuse her without losing his job. She couldn't take advantage of the poor man. Or could she? *Gigolo*. Why had Sylvie used that old-fashioned term? And why was the thought of having Zachary fill that role so appealing?

Losing her steady beau had left a hole in her life, one that she'd thought she would be in no hurry to fill. But, as she'd been forced to admit to Sylvie—and to herself—she *needed* a man. Maybe it wasn't so strange that she'd like to get the man on her own terms. But turn her personal assistant into a gigolo? Not likely. Betancourt Coffees had a very strict policy against sexual harassment.

With an emphatic shake of her head, Chloe said, "No, I couldn't do that."

"You could. You don't want to. Probably doing such a thing offends your Southern lady sensibilities. But remember, sweetie, I've known you since you took over this business when you were barely out of your teens. I've seen you nose to nose with longshoremen. If you can order big bruisers like them to handle your precious coffee beans with care, you can order that man to go out with you."

"You're right, I could. I don't want to," she said, not as forcefully as she'd intended. "Besides, he probably doesn't own a tuxedo," she added lamely.

"You could rent him one."

"I don't know." Chloe frowned, feeling her resolve weakening. "He's so agreeable, he would probably do it if I asked. But he's not very...forceful. I'm not sure if he'd be much help."

"You need a man, remember? And you don't have time to be choosy."

In the outer office, Zach ground his teeth together in frustration. Thanks to modern technology and a court-ordered wiretap, he could hear every word the two women uttered. The earphones he wore received the transmissions from the bugs he and the tech agent had planted in Chloe Betancourt's office, and they also worked with the Dictaphone.

Agreeable he could live with—his subservient act was just that, an act. But *scrawny?* Come on, ladies! He might be a few pounds under his normal weight, enough that his clothes hung loosely from his shoulders, but he was far from a ninety-pound weakling. A few more weeks of eating shrimp and oyster po'boys dripping with mayo, and he would regain all the weight he'd lost. And it wouldn't be fat, either. Zach had set himself a grueling exercise regimen to build up his wasted muscles, and he'd performed it faithfully every day since he'd been released from the rehabilitation clinic. He'd progressed far enough that his limp was faked. Most of the time. He'd only kept it because it fit with the undercover persona he'd created for the job.

Taking a deep breath, Zach admitted that his boss's reluctance to ask him out stung—and not just on a professional level. The fact that he'd barely seen her for the first two weeks of his assignment rankled. Still, he knew he would find a way to get close to her, with or without her cooperation. No, his problem wasn't only professional, it was personal.

Zach wanted Chloe to want to be with him.

That was not good. Not for the investigation, or the investigator. He had to stay objective. If he let Chloe get to him, he'd be looking for ways to clear her of suspicion.

And too many clues pointed to her.

Item one: Chloe Betancourt's father had amassed

an impressive collection of pre-Columbian art and artifacts before his death. He'd left his collection and his company to his wife and daughter, along with a pile of unpaid bills. The collection had disappeared soon after, apparently sold to keep the company afloat. So Chloe knew about pre-Columbian art, having learned at her father's knee. She'd know the value of individual pieces, and she had probably learned who the avid collectors were when she'd sold her father's collection.

Item two: a year and a half ago, Chloe had traveled to Caldas, Colombia, to negotiate a contract with Alejandro Velásquez, the owner of a coffee estate conveniently located next to a recently discovered pre-Columbian archeological site, one of the few to be discovered in Colombia. Shortly after Chloe signed the agreement with the Velásquez coffee plantation, artifacts began disappearing from the site.

Item three: Chloe Betancourt—

The door to the inner office opened, interrupting Zach's review of the evidence. Sylvie Sheridan walked out of Chloe's office, followed by his petite boss. The two women appeared to be good friends, but he hadn't figured out the reason. Sylvie was older by at least ten years, making it unlikely that they'd met at school. Their styles weren't anything alike. Sylvie dressed like a carnival fortune-teller, while Chloe favored severely tailored suits.

Today's suit was the same shade of blue as her eyes, with a long jacket and a short skirt. Zach let his gaze slide down her legs. He still hadn't figured out how a woman only an inch or two over five feet could have such long, elegant legs. She probably thought her wardrobe made her look as tough as she thought she was, but her suits couldn't completely disguise her soft, womanly curves. Chloe Betancourt might think of herself as an Amazon, but anyone with half a brain could see she was the kind of woman who needed a man's protection.

No matter how attractive she was, Zach thanked his lucky star that Ms. Chloe Betancourt didn't have any real power over him—a woman with her attitude toward the male sex was a woman to be avoided. His inappropriate attraction to her had to have its roots in some primitive desire to show her how a man and woman were meant to relate.

But some other man would have to do that job.

Duty, not desire, demanded that he keep company with her. Close company. Something he'd been unable to do during his first weeks on the job. Ms. Betancourt spent a lot of time out of the office—at the warehouse where the raw coffee beans were stored, in the building where the beans were roasted, ground and packaged, or in the kitchens where new blends were brewed and tasted.

Zach had to find a way to get close to her.

For the sake of the investigation.

"Thanks for the coffee, Chloe. It was the best, as always. Maybe you should think about opening your own chain of coffeehouses. Then you wouldn't have to charm Mr. Cox."

"One company's enough for me. More than enough."

Zach was surprised at her wistful tone. He knew she'd been running the company since her father's untimely death eight years previously. Her dossier, plus the tapes he'd listened to of her conversations, had given him the definite feeling that she liked being in control.

Chloe added, "I'll see you Thursday at the Chamber of Commerce luncheon."

"Fine." Fastening her cape at the throat, Sylvie stopped by Zach's desk. "Nice to meet you, Mr. Steele. Don't let Chloe push you around."

Zach lowered his eyes. "No, ma'am." He jerked his head up and gave Chloe a nervous look. "I—I mean, she can push me around if she wants to. She is the boss."

Sylvie grinned. "Have fun, you two. Bye." She left the room with a flourish.

"Bye." Chloe turned back to her office.

"Ms. Betancourt? I couldn't help overhearing...that you need a man this evening. An escort, I mean."

She looked at him over her shoulder, her eyes narrowing suspiciously. "Yes."

Fumbling with a stack of invoices, Zach cleared his throat. "I wouldn't mind working overtime."

"Excuse me?"

"If you think I'd do, that is." Zach tugged at the collar of his shirt, although it wasn't tight. He wanted to convey a certain...diffident nervousness. He'd already learned that Chloe was wary of men. Office gossip put it down to her stormy relationship with her father, and the remarks he'd just overheard corroborated that theory. "Never mind, I shouldn't have been so bold." He turned back to the invoices, tapping them into a neat stack.

"No, wait." She walked back to stand in front of his desk. "You took me by surprise, that's all. I do need an escort. And since you're volunteering, I'd be happy for you to take me to the reception tonight."

"Fine," Zach said, looking up at her. Too bad he hadn't mastered the art of blushing on demand.

"You don't happen to own a tuxedo, do you?"

"Yes. I had to buy one for my sister's wedding." Zach didn't have a sister. He made a mental note to add one to his undercover persona's biography.

"Well, then, that's fine. We're all set. The reception is at seven. I live in the Cotton Warehouse, just down the street, on the fourth floor. You can pick me up at six-thirty. Unless... Should I pick you up?"

Zach shook his head. "No, ma'am. I'll come for you."

"Take a cab and have it wait. The reception is in the French Quarter, and we don't want to waste time finding a place to park. I'll reimburse you for the taxi, of course."

"I won't need a cab to get to your place—I live in the Warehouse District, too."

"Mr. Steele. Warehouse District? We don't call it

that any longer. Warehouses are not politically correct, you know. Now it's the Arts District." Many of the old buildings upriver from the French Quarter and New Orleans's central business district had been converted into apartments, condominiums and art galleries. The Contemporary Arts Center was just around the corner from Betancourt Coffees's warehouse and offices.

"Oh. Sorry. I didn't know."

"I was teasing, Zachary. As a matter of fact—and don't tell Sylvie I said this—I think Arts District is just the teeniest bit pretentious. Since you don't need a taxi to get to my apartment, tell the doorman to call one as soon as you get there."

"Yes, Ms. Betancourt," Zach said.

Zach rang the doorbell at Chloe's condominium promptly at six-thirty. He'd almost been late, not realizing he would have to climb three flights of stairs to reach her apartment. A building that boasted a doorman ought to have an elevator, to his way of thinking. He'd taken the stairs slowly, to avoid arriving at Chloe's door with his tongue hanging out.

Chloe opened the door. Zach's eyes bugged out. She wondered why men pawed and panted over her? Yeah, sure. Any woman who looked like her, and who had her money to boot, had to know she'd attract men like jasmine attracted bees. Especially in the outfit she was wearing. The honey-colored dress matched her skintones so perfectly that for a heart-stopping moment he'd thought she hadn't been dressed. "That's what you're wearing?" he blurted.

She raised an eyebrow. "Yes. You look nice. Come in, Zachary."

"So do you," he mumbled, stumbling a little as he stepped over the threshold.

"Oh, I should have remembered your limp. There is a freight elevator in the back of the building. Frank could have brought you up in that."

"No problem. I'm supposed to exercise the leg."

"What happened? Were you in an accident?"

"Yes." He'd accidentally gotten in the way of a couple of bullets.

"Please, come in."

Zach walked into the large, high-ceilinged room and looked around. No electronic surveillance equipment had been placed in Chloe's home—not enough probable cause to get a warrant. The P.C. the agency had come up with so far was limited to her business. But if he observed any evidence of smuggling in the apartment, he could write up a new affidavit and they could try again.

The brick walls weren't the backdrop for any expensive artwork. Only colorful posters from various Louisiana festivals decorated the walls. That only meant Chloe Betancourt was smart enough not to flaunt her booty. She could be the kind of collector who kept her artifacts in a secret vault somewhere. Or, if she was the middleman, selling to other collectors, she could be stashing her profits in a Swiss bank account.

A glass display case between the windows caught his eye, but closer inspection revealed only a collection of coffee mugs. No pre-Columbian artifacts in view. Not that he'd expected any. That would have made his job too easy.

"Would you like a drink?" Chloe asked, moving to a bar tucked in the corner of the large room.

Zach looked at his watch. "Do we have time?"

"We'll make time. I think we need to get a few things straight before we leave. Is white wine all right?"

"Yes, ma'am."

"Don't call me ma'am, Zachary."

"Oh, yeah. I guess I wouldn't call a date ma'am."

"No, but this is not a date." She took a chilled bottle of Chablis from the tiny refrigerator under the bar, removed the cork and poured two glasses.

Zach accepted one of the glasses and took a sip. "I knew that, too. A woman like you wouldn't go out with someone like me. This is business."

"Right. Business." She eyed him over the rim of her wineglass. "'A woman like me'? What does that mean?"

"Uh. Well, I mean you're the boss, and I'm...not. I'm the one getting paid overtime for this evening."

"Yes. Time and a half." For some reason she turned pink when she mentioned his payment for the evening.

Zach suppressed a grin. If paying for an escort made her blush, maybe Chloe wasn't quite the Amazon she professed to be. "Great. I could use the money. Doctors' bills."

"Are you sure you're up to a late evening?"

Now she looked worried. Her concern warmed him, and Zach found himself wanting to smooth away the tiny lines furrowing her brow. With his mouth. He gulped down the rest of the wine. "Yes, Ms. Betancourt. I'm fully recovered from my accident."

"Well, if you get tired, be sure and let me know. I don't want to cause a relapse."

"That's very kind of you," he said stiffly, fighting the urge to show her just how recovered he was.

"And if a chore like this should be necessary in the future, please don't feel obligated to accept my invitation. I know you volunteered this time, but if I had asked you, you would have been perfectly free to say no."

"I don't mind working late. Like I said, I can use the money, Ms. Betancourt."

She set her glass on the counter. "You can't call me Ms. Betancourt, either. We want other people to *think* you're my date. Call me Chloe. And I suppose you'd better act like you're interested in me."

Zach drew his brows together in a puzzled frown. "Interested? How?"

"The way men do. You know." She walked around the bar to stand next to him.

She was close now. Too close. He could smell her

perfume, musky and mysterious. His collar, which had been loose like all his collars, suddenly seemed too tight. "I'm not sure I do." Sliding off the bar stool, he forced himself to move even closer to her—just to prove to himself that he could resist her. "Should I hold your hand? Touch you?"

"No." She backed up a step. Good. Being next to him bothered her. "Yes. I don't mean that you should paw me in public, Zachary. But a few discreet touches would be appropriate. The main thing I want you to do is to stick close to me. Keep other men away—especially anyone named Arcenaux. But not Mr. Cox. He's the guest of honor, the man I want to talk business with."

"I got it. I can do that." Inching forward another step, Zach smothered a grin when she backed up again. He knew better than to play games with a target, but he could take only so much of acting the subservient male, especially when being around Chloe made him feel primitive and powerful.

"Good. Now that we've got that straight, I'll get my coat and we'll be off. Did you ask Frank to call us a taxi?" She turned her bare back on him and reached for a short satin coat hanging on the hall tree.

"Allow me," said Zach, taking the coat and holding it for her. "Who's Frank? Oh, the doorman. Yes. He said he'd have one waiting."

Chloe slid her arms into the coat, and Zach let his hands rest a moment longer than necessary on her shoulders. He felt her tremble and immediately dropped his hands. Chloe Betancourt attracted him, no doubt about it. And that tremor he'd just felt could mean that the attraction was mutual. Not that it mattered one way or another, because duty would keep him from going too far down that road. Only a fool would risk compromising an investigation for something as fleeting as sexual attraction.

Zach was no fool.

2

Chloe gave the address of the hotel to the cabdriver and settled back. So far, so good. Zachary looked great in a tuxedo, even if it did fit him a bit loosely. He was taller than Mark, by several inches. Normally she did not like men who towered above her, but Zachary's six-foot-plus frame did not seem threatening. Maybe because his limp made him appear vulnerable. The important thing was that he'd accepted her instructions without a lot of questions or criticisms. Chloe liked the way he took orders, without even a hint that he resented having a woman as his boss. And Zachary not only took orders well, he executed them faultlessly.

When they arrived, she started to open the cab door.

Zach touched her arm. "Wait. I'll get that for you." He got out of the cab and hurried to open her door for her.

"Thank you, Zachary," she said, smiling. His old-fashioned manners reminded her that men did have their uses. If her luck held, Zachary would be as good at keeping other men at bay as he was at opening doors. That might be asking too much of him—Zachary was more self-effacing than self-confident. Oh, well, it was too late to worry about that now.

After checking her wrap, Chloe took his arm and led him to the ballroom where the reception was being held. The first familiar face she saw was her nemesis.

"Not alone this evening, I see," said Emile Arcenaux, looking Zach over. "New boyfriend?"

"This is Zachary Steele," said Chloe, ignoring Emile's smirk. "Zachary, Emile and Bette Arcenaux." Zach might be perfect, but everything wasn't going her way—not if she'd ended up behind her rival in the receiving line.

"It won't be enough, you know," Emile said.

"Excuse me?" said Chloe.

"A boyfriend won't cut it with Cox. He's big on family life. Very big. Requires all his executives to be married. His suppliers, too, from what I hear."

"Surely not," Chloe murmured. Emile was up to his good-old-boy tricks, trying to put her on the defensive because she was a woman and, therefore, not suited to the rough and tumble of the business world. "I'm sure Mr. Cox must want the best product available."

"Of course. But all things being equal...I'm betting that he'll prefer to do business with a devout family man over a man-hating spinster." With a smug smile, Emile placed his arm around his wife's waist and pulled her close just as they reached the guest of honor. "Mr. Cox. Emile Arcenaux. Creole Coffees. And this is the little woman, Bette."

Chloe almost gagged. Emile Arcenaux was a notorious womanizer, and here he was playing doting husband. "Good grief," she groaned. She could tell by the way Cox beamed at the couple that he was falling for the act.

Emile and his wife finally moved on. "Welcome to New Orleans, Mr. Cox. I'm Chloe Betancourt, and this is Zachary Steele, my—"

"Fiancé," said Zachary, shaking Mr. Cox's hand.

Chloe's mouth dropped open. With a grin, Zachary touched her chin, closing it. Zachary continued, "Sorry, darling. I know we haven't announced our engagement publicly yet, but Mr. Cox looks like a man who can keep a secret."

"I sure am." Mr. Cox took Chloe's hand in both of his. "Congratulations, my dear. What's the reason for the secrecy, anyway?"

Recovering quickly, Chloe said, "My mother. She's in Europe for a few months, and I wanted her to be the first to know." She glared at Zachary.

Chuckling, Gerald Cox patted her hand. "Don't be too hard on him, young lady. Any man worth his salt wants to stake his claim as soon as he finds his woman. And he's right about me, Miss Betancourt. I am a man who knows when to keep his mouth shut. We'll talk later, as soon as this receiving line business is finished. I knew your father, you know."

As soon as they were out of the guest of honor's earshot, Chloe rounded on Zachary. "What on earth possessed you, Zachary Steele? You told Gerald Cox you were my fiancé. Right out of the blue, no warning at all. How could you do that?''

His brow wrinkled, making him look like a little boy caught with his hand in the cookie jar. Chloe almost reached out her hand to smooth away the worry before she realized what she was doing. Tapping her foot instead, she said, "Well? Explain yourself."

"I can't. It just popped out. I'm really sorry, Ms. Betancourt. What can I do to correct my mistake? Do you want me to tell him I lied?"

"Yes!" Chloe took a deep breath. "Maybe." She needed time to think this through, and she wasn't going to get it. Two of Emile's bulky cousins were headed their way. "No. We'll discuss this later," she snapped. "We've got company."

"Dance, Miss Chloe?" asked Steve Arcenaux, shouldering past Zachary.

"Would you like something to drink, Chloe, honey?" Steve's brother, Richard, suggested.

"This dance is mine," said Zach forcefully. He stepped between Steve and Chloe and took her by the hand. "But you can get us both a glass of champagne. We'll meet you back here after the dance." With that, he whirled her onto the dance floor, leaving Steve and Richard with their mouths hanging open.

Chloe felt her chin about to drop again, too. What had happened to her sweet, subservient personal assistant? He had managed to rout the Arcenaux brothers in the blink of an eye, and he'd done it without shouting or bloodshed. For a moment there, her scrawny secretary had transformed himself into a dangerous and imposing protector.

Zachary had stood a couple of inches taller than the Arcenauxs, and his shoulders were broader than theirs. But Chloe didn't think it was Zachary's size that had intimidated Steve and Richard so effectively.

It was his attitude. Where had that arrogant self-confidence come from?

She almost thanked him, until she recalled what else he'd done. "Really, Zachary! Whatever possessed you to tell Mr. Cox we're engaged? I know you haven't worked for me very long, so maybe you aren't used to my management style. Still, I thought I made your duties for the evening very clear."

"You did. I'm to stay close, keep everyone except Mr. Cox away, and act like I'm interested in you."

"'Interested' is a long way from engaged. What made you think I needed a fiancé? I certainly didn't expect you to be so...spontaneous. Not to mention reckless. I'm extremely annoyed with you." She didn't sound annoyed, she sounded breathless. Perhaps now, when she was being held in Zachary's surprisingly strong arms, wasn't the best time to deliver a lecture. But she couldn't let his mutiny go unchallenged.

"I am sorry, Chloe. I can't explain why I said what I said. Except that Arcenaux guy got to me, making those cracks about you being a man-hater. You're not like that. You're warm and considerate and a wonderful boss. I only wanted to help."

He sounded so mortified and looked so contrite, Chloe felt her anger fading. With a brisk nod, she said, "All right. I forgive you. We'll just have to make the best of it. At least you said it was a secret engagement. We can break it off as soon as Mr. Cox leaves town, and no one will be the wiser." After a pause, she added grudgingly, "And you did handle the Arcenaux boys very well."

"Thank you, Miss Chloe, honey," he said, a mischievous gleam in his eye as he mimicked Steve and Richard. "I aim to please." He pulled her a fraction of an inch closer.

"You shouldn't have told them we'd meet them after the dance, though." Zachary had sounded just the teeniest bit smug. Perhaps she'd let him off the hook too soon. Any good manager knew that tendencies toward insubordination needed to be nipped firmly in the bud.

"We aren't meeting them. I lied."

"Oh. You sounded sincere."

"I meant to. I don't believe in doing something unless I can do it well," said Zachary. "Including telling lies. I see Mr. Cox. Shall we dance his way?"

"Yes."

Zachary efficiently negotiated the width of the dance floor, ending up next to the table where Gerald Cox and his party were seated.

"Ah, there you are. I see you haven't made it to the bar yet. What can I get for you?" asked Cox as he stood to hold a chair out for Chloe.

"Please sit down, Mr. Cox. I'll attend to drinks," said Zachary. "Chablis, dear?"

Chloe nodded. Zachary had no more trouble mouthing endearments than telling lies. Her personal assistant was full of surprises this evening. "Yes, please, darling," she returned. She could play a part, too.

"Mr. Cox? What's your pleasure?"

"Scotch. Rocks. Don't hurry back. I'd like to talk to Miss Betancourt about her father's art collection."

Zachary hesitated, then shrugged and headed for the bar. Chloe didn't have time to wonder why he'd suddenly seemed reluctant to leave her. She had Gerald Cox all to herself.

"Well, now, young lady. When's the wedding date?"

"What wedding—oh, you mean mine and Zachary's. We haven't set one yet. As we told you, we haven't even announced our engagement."

"Because your mother is out of the country. Will she be returning soon?"

"Not for several months. She's on an educational tour sponsored by the University of New Orleans. Sort of a semester abroad."

"Well, don't wait too long. Your Zachary may lose patience and take matters into his own hands."

"Zachary won't do anything until I—until *we* decide on a mutually satisfactory date. Now, Mr. Cox—"

"Call me Gerald, my dear. I feel like an old family friend."

"Oh, yes. You said you knew my father."

"Not well, but our paths crossed a few times. I first met him at an auction of pre-Columbian art. Fortunately, we weren't after the same thing. He preferred pottery, while I only collect gold and silver artifacts. But we had a common passion for the San Agustín culture of Colombia. I was sorry to hear of his passing."

"Thank you," Chloe murmured. "It happened a long time ago."

"You've done a good job keeping his company in the forefront of the specialty coffee market. Quite a coup you pulled, signing an exclusive contract with the Velásquez farm. I'm very impressed. Only a bright entrepreneur would have seen that estate coffees are the wave of the future. My marketing people tell me before long we'll all be buying coffee the same way we buy wine."

"That's what I'm betting on. What are your plans, Mr. Cox? Will you be opening your Coffee Emporiums in New Orleans?"

"I haven't decided yet. I'd like to expand, but the bean counters are telling me to slow down. For now, it's an excuse to spend time in one of my favorite cities. Marian—that's Mrs. Cox—will be joining me in a day or two. She's coming by yacht from Florida."

"She sails?"

Chuckling, Gerald Cox patted her on the hand. "Not alone. We have a crew. Marian wants to cruise up the Mississippi to Natchez. She plans to visit the antebellum homes along the river. They'll be decorated for Christmas, won't they?"

"Yes. And this time of year you can see the bonfires being constructed on the levees."

"Ah, I've heard of that. They light them on Christmas Eve to show Papa Noël the way."

"That's right. It's quite a sight."

"Well, we'll have to be back in Florida before Christmas Eve. But if we can't see the bonfires burning, we can at least see them being constructed. Perhaps you and your fiancé will join us?"

"How kind of you to ask," Chloe murmured, not sure if she wanted to take the fake engagement that far.

"I'll get back to you on the departure date. In the meantime, I'd like to look over your operation. When might I visit Betancourt Coffees?"

"Anytime."

"Monday, then."

Zachary returned with their drinks at the same time other guests converged on the table. Chloe rose gracefully and said, "Thank you for your time, Mr. Cox— Gerald. I mustn't monopolize the guest of honor, however. Zachary, perhaps we should leave now."

"I'll have the doorman call us a cab."

"Taxi? No need for that. My car is out front, and I won't be needing it for several hours. I'm taking a few close friends to dinner just around the corner, at Antoine's."

Gerald Cox was on his feet and ushering them toward the exit before Chloe could stop him. Pausing briefly at the hatcheck counter to recover her evening coat, Zachary took Chloe by the arm as they followed the man out the door of the hotel. Cox signaled one of the drivers lounging against a long black limousine. He opened the door and waited until Chloe and Zachary were settled in the back seat.

"Roger, take these folks wherever they want to go. And take your time. Meet me at the restaurant later. No rush—not for me, anyway. But from the look on Zachary's face, he may be in something of a hurry. Maybe you'd better close the window and give them a little privacy." Chuckling, he closed the door and waved them on their way.

The driver obeyed orders, raising the barrier between the driver's seat and the back of the limousine.

Chloe sat on the edge of the seat, suddenly nervous. Everything seemed to be conspiring to bring her and her new assistant together on a personal level. First, her own unbusinesslike fantasizing about her new employee, then Sylvie talking about gigolos and suggesting that she could order Zachary to act as her escort. Next, his volunteering to do that very thing. Now Gerald Cox sending them on a romantic ride through the French Quarter in a limousine with smoked-glass windows and a moon roof.

Maybe she should take advantage—not of Zachary, but of the situation. She would never force herself on him, but she could try a little experiment. She wouldn't go too far, only far enough to see if that quickly hidden yearning she thought she'd observed in a few of his glances was real. Thanks to Zachary, she had a perfectly good excuse. They were engaged.

Aware that her pulse had sped up noticeably, Chloe peeked at Zachary out of the corner of her eye. He looked at ease, lounging against the back of the seat, his long legs stretched out in front of him and crossed at the ankles. She cleared her throat, but couldn't think of anything to say.

"What kind of art collection did your father have?" asked Zachary.

"What? How did you know about that?"

"Mr. Cox mentioned it."

"Oh, yes. Father collected local Louisiana artists, for the most part. He'd buy when they were hungry, and hold their works until they appreciated in value. Art was business to my father." Everything had been business to her father. And he hadn't dropped his controlling ways at home, either. He'd micromanaged her mother's every move, and he'd tried to do the same with her. She and her father had had some spectacular clashes when she was growing up.

"Are the posters in your apartment part of his collection?"

"No. I picked those up at various festivals around the state. Betancourt Coffees tries to have a presence at local events, like the Strawberry Festival in Ponchatoula. Dad never would have fooled around with something as common as posters."

"Where is his collection? At your mother's house?"

"Not there, either. Mother and I had to sell most

of the collection after he died. That's how I met Sylvie. She handled the sales for us. Zachary, did you tell the driver my address?"

"No." He leaned forward to tap on the glass divider.

Chloe grabbed his hand. "Not yet. Are you in a hurry to get home?"

"N-no, I guess not."

Chloe grinned and scooted closer to Zachary. He sounded nervous, more in character. Just as she'd thought, his earlier bold behavior had been an aberration—probably brought on by that very same nervousness.

"How did Mr. Cox know your father?" Zachary asked.

"As it turns out, he and my father attended the same auctions from time to time, looking for items to add to their collections." She rested her hand gently on his knee. "This is nice, isn't it?"

"Cox is interested in Louisiana artists?" Zachary lifted her hand off his knee and moved closer to the passenger door.

Chloe followed, suddenly feeling like Diana the huntress. She liked the feeling. "No, pre-Columbian art. My father collected that, too. New Orleans is the port of entry for a lot of immigrants and visitors from South America. Some of them bring artifacts with them."

"I thought our neighbors to the south frowned on the export of their national treasures."

"They do. Now, exporting such things is against

the law in most of the Latin American countries. It was legal when my father accumulated his collection, however."

"Who bought his pre-Columbian art?"

"Zachary, I don't want to talk about my father's art collection." She placed her hand on his thigh and squeezed gently. "If we're going to be engaged, I think we should practice."

"Practice? Practice what?" His voice sounded strangled. He moved her hand again.

She ran her hand down his arm. "Being engaged. Mr. Cox will expect us to act like we're in love."

"I thought you were going to tell him I lied about the engagement."

"I changed my mind. Emile was right. Mr. Cox is very big on family. Your little white lie turned out to be just what he needed to hear. I'm afraid Mr. Cox is of the old school, and something of a chauvinist. He wouldn't have given a strong, independent woman the time of day. Kiss me, Zachary."

He actually jumped. "What? Is that really necessary? Mr. Cox isn't around now."

"His chauffeur is. And Mr. Cox will be soon. He's visiting the company on Monday." Chloe swung her legs over Zachary's and climbed onto his lap. "We have to get used to touching one another, Zachary, or he'll figure out that something's wrong. You're the one who got us engaged, after all. Or did you forget that?"

Tugging on his collar, Zachary said, "No. But—"

"No buts. Let me fix that for you." Chloe untied

his bow tie, and unbuttoned the top two buttons of his shirt. "There, that's better." Having a fiancé, especially one on the payroll, was as close as she would ever get to having her very own gigolo. She couldn't pass up this opportunity. "Kiss me, Zachary," she ordered in her best C.E.O. voice.

"I beg your pardon?" He tugged at the collar of his shirt.

"I said, kiss me. Now." She closed her eyes and tilted her head back.

"Why?"

Chloe opened her eyes. She supposed she could forgive his reluctance. He'd only volunteered to be her escort, not her boy toy. But he had assumed the role of fiancé. He couldn't blame her for that. She wrapped her arms around his neck. "You have to kiss me, Zachary. It's bound to come up, sooner or later. Mr. Cox will expect you to kiss me at some point—especially since we may go on a cruise on his yacht. We'd better try it a few times, so we won't be awkward when we have to do it in front of him." She lowered her voice to a husky whisper. "Besides, his driver may report back to him."

Her heart was pounding so hard, she was sure he must hear it. And her expression had to be giving her away. This was no experiment. Chloe wanted desperately for Zachary to kiss her. She'd never wanted anything more.

Because her father, the man she'd known best, had been a domineering man, one who treated his "little woman" with contempt, Chloe had never allowed any of her beaux, Mark included, to get too close. But this was different. Zachary was different.

The idea of a man totally and completely under her control had been growing in appeal ever since she and Sylvie had discussed it. It had quickly become an obsession. And Zachary couldn't claim sexual harassment—not after he'd taken it upon himself to announce their engagement.

"All right, Ms. Betancourt—Chloe. I'll kiss you." He turned slightly and pecked her on the cheek.

"That's the best you can do?"

Zachary glanced toward the driver. "He can't see us. This isn't necessary."

"I'll be the judge of that. I demand that you kiss me properly. Not that I expect you to use your tongue, Zachary. Mr. Cox wouldn't expect that, either, not in public. But kiss me on the mouth, at least." She closed her eyes and puckered up again.

"This is not a good idea," he muttered right before his mouth touched hers. Zach kept his lips pressed tightly together. She had said no tongue. The little shrew hadn't meant it. Her soft lips were parting, and she was using her tongue to trace his lower lip.

Groaning, Zach jerked his head up. He couldn't lose control. Chloe knew more than she ought to know about the international laws against smuggling. That alone would keep her firmly in the "target" category. And he'd seen her make contact with a wealthy collector of pre-Columbian art. For all he knew, they could have been arranging a transaction right under his nose. He never should have left them alone.

Chloe nuzzled his neck, planting small kisses on his exposed throat. Zach tried pushing her away. She didn't budge. His petite boss was stronger than she looked. "Chloe. Ms. Betancourt. Stop," he said weakly.

"Not yet. Kiss me again, Zachary."

He caught her under the knees and moved her off his lap. "No. I'm not that kind of man."

"What kind of man?"

"You know. Easy."

"I know that. This isn't real, Zachary. It's a charade. For Mr. Cox's benefit, remember?"

Zach crossed his arms over his chest and stared out the window. "Mr. Cox isn't here. His chauffeur can't see us. This is not necessary."

"I think it is. But I don't want to make you uncomfortable. I realize our engagement may take some getting used to. Let this be a lesson, Zachary. Look before you leap. You felt sorry for me, and let your emotions speak for you. Now you're stuck with being my gig—fiancé until Mr. Cox leaves town." She patted him on the knee. "We'll practice more later. You may tell the driver we're ready to go home."

Keeping his face averted so that Chloe wouldn't see his scowl, Zach leaned forward and tapped on the glass. The shield opened. "Cotton Warehouse, corner of Julia and Tchoupitoulas."

Zach didn't offer to escort Chloe up the stairs to her door. He left her with the doorman and returned to the limousine. No telling what she'd decide they had to practice if she got him inside her apartment.

Dismissing the driver, he walked the few blocks to his place. The breeze blowing off the river made the temperature cool enough that it should do the work of a cold shower.

He'd call the office and leave a voice mail message to have Gerald Cox checked out. If some of the smuggled goods turned up in his collection, they'd be a long way toward winding up this investigation.

A picture of Chloe behind bars flashed through his mind. He didn't like thinking about that. She put up a tough front, but he had reason to know how soft and vulnerable she really was. He'd felt her response to his reluctant kiss. She would have gone up in flames if he'd been a little more willing to "practice."

Swearing, Zach told himself not to care about what happened to Chloe. If she'd violated the law, she had to suffer the consequences. That was the way it worked. He had to make the case against her, but her fate after that would be out of his hands.

In the meantime he'd have to find a way to stay out of her hands.

And he would make the case against her. That was his job. He was good at what he did.

Yeah, right. So good, he'd gotten himself shot the last time out. And now—his clever ploy of identifying himself as Chloe's future husband had backfired. Big time. The woman who'd said only that morning that she hated needing a man had embraced her bride-to-be role enthusiastically. No way he could have predicted that.

He hadn't anticipated practice kisses, either. Zach's lower lip twitched as he remembered her soft little tongue tracing its shape. He could still taste her.

Zach pushed open the door to his apartment building and headed for the stairs. No more elevators for him. Punishing exercise sessions and cold showers would get him through the next few weeks. He had never compromised an investigation for a quick roll in the hay, and he never would. Forget that Chloe Betancourt, C.E.O., was an attractive, vibrant, sexy woman. She was the prime suspect of his investigation.

He'd found a way to stay close to her. He would just have to make sure he didn't get too close for comfort.

3

Engaged.

Chloe's first thought on waking Saturday morning brought a smile to her face. Why hadn't she thought of a fake engagement? Zachary, bless him, had come up with the perfect solution to her problem. A fiancé was even better than a steady beau at keeping other men at bay. Especially men with hidden agendas, like the Arcenauxs.

Too bad it couldn't last. Zachary was only a temporary employee, after all. Three months and he'd be gone.

She rolled over and buried her face in her pillow. Three months could be long enough. If Betancourt Coffees got the Cox's Coffee Emporium contract, the company would be operating at near full capacity. She could relax for the first time since she'd had to take over the helm of the family company.

Remembering the hectic weeks following her father's untimely death, Chloe burrowed deeper under the covers. Unprepared and grieving, she had never been so afraid in her life. But she'd gotten through it, hour by hour, day by day, faking knowledge she hadn't had and projecting confidence she hadn't felt.

Thanks to the few business classes she'd worked into her curriculum at Tulane, and a big dose of on-the-job training, she'd managed to keep her head above water. She'd done well enough, in fact, that she had almost conquered her fear of failure. But still, every once in a while...

She could be in the middle of negotiating a contract or bidding on new business, and it would happen. She'd get that panicky I-can't-do-this feeling. Her mind would go blank and she'd forget to breathe. Quaking inside, she'd look around, expecting to see her father stride into the room, pat her on the head, and send her off to play with her dolls.

She'd learned to deal with it. She would take calming breaths, smile at her customer, and get on with business. No doubt about it, her confidence had grown over the years, but she hadn't completely conquered her fears. She needed one more success before she could relax, and becoming the Louisiana supplier for Cox's Coffee Emporiums could be it.

The Cox contract would put Betancourt Coffees's bottom line firmly in the black. Chloe fervently hoped that success would end her qualms and quakes once and for all.

Then she would be able to enjoy a few social events without worrying about schmoozing with present and potential customers. She could even stay at home and curl up with a good book—or a good man—and not feel guilty about taking time for herself.

Rolling onto her back, Chloe stretched her arms over her head, grinning. Time for herself. Time to do the things she liked for the sheer joy of doing them— not because they were necessary, or prudent, or good business. After eight years of struggling to make it in her father's world, she'd finally reached a place from where she could see the top. She'd get there yet. She knew it.

Stretching her arms again, Chloe smiled. Making that final push to the summit could wait a while. While she had Zachary on the payroll, she could experiment with another kind of personal growth. She'd devoted the last eight years to business. It was past time for her to learn about her passion quotient. Except for the lukewarm liaison with her old reliable, Mark Michelet, she hadn't had time or energy for a relationship. Even if she'd had time, she hadn't wanted any permanent commitment.

With a shudder, she acknowledged that she still didn't want that. Chloe had promised herself that she would never again let a man tell her what she could and could not do. Her father's domineering pronouncements on the role of women had almost destroyed Betancourt Coffees, and her along with it.

When she'd expressed an interest in learning the business as a teenager, her father had scoffed. He'd told her that business was no place for a woman. Women were too weak, too indecisive, too *nice* to succeed as entrepreneurs. Having those paternal precepts echoing in her ears had almost sunk her when she'd needed every ounce of self-confidence she could muster.

As much as she would have liked to blame all her problems on her father, Chloe couldn't do that. She'd made some spectacular mistakes all on her own. In an immature fit of rebellion, she'd decided to major in French literature. A wiser course would have been to tell her father if she couldn't count on taking over the family business, she'd just start her own. Then she could have done the sensible thing and gotten her degree in business administration. As it was, her expensive education had been useless when she'd had to deal with creditors and suppliers and customers.

But her degree might have its uses now. A woman with a lover might find need for the thin volumes of French poetry tucked in her bookcases. French was the language of seduction, after all.

Lover? Did she really want to take her experiment that far? She'd told Sylvie she could do without sex. But, as Sylvie had shrewdly pointed out, why should she? With Zachary, she'd be in charge. He was a rarity, a man who didn't want to be in control.

Zachary was only temporarily in her life. She might never again have the opportunity to have an attractive man at her beck and call. And the best part was, Zachary had volunteered for the after-hours job. He'd even come up with a better role to play than the one she'd fantasized about.

Fiancé had a much classier ring to it than *gigolo*. Semantics aside, if she handled the situation with finesse, she could have Zachary right where she wanted him.

Which was where, exactly?

What would a man do with a secretary he found attractive and intriguing? As Sylvie had pointed out, Zachary was shy. Sylvie found that exciting. So did Chloe. A man who didn't use his masculinity to intimidate and overpower a woman was very appealing.

If their positions were reversed, Zachary would seduce her, of course.

Next question: how did a man go about seducing a woman? Chin in hand, Chloe reviewed her dating experiences. A man who was interested in a woman flattered her. He sent her flowers. He took her to dinner and plied her with wine. He danced with her, holding her closer than absolutely necessary. He touched her at every opportunity. He kissed her deeply, passionately—

No. That could take months, and she only had weeks. A man's way would take much too long. She'd do it her way. She'd be direct and straightforward. She'd make very clear what she wanted right up front. She certainly didn't want to give Zachary the impression that her intentions were anything but dishonorable. She wanted an affair, plain and simple. A brief, satisfying, *safe* affair.

Suddenly energized, Chloe threw back the covers and leaped out of bed. She had to go to the office to check on the progress of the container ship with its precious cargo. She could order—ask Zachary to join her there.

In the adjoining bathroom, Chloe pulled her nightshirt over her head. Saturday was Zachary's day off, but he had volunteered to work unlimited overtime. He did need to see the complete operation before Gerald Cox appeared on Monday for his tour of the company. As her fiancé, Zachary would be expected to know more about the business than her filing system. Tossing the nightshirt into the clothes hamper, Chloe walked into the glass-enclosed shower and turned on the water.

The message light on her answering machine was blinking when she returned to the bedroom after her shower. The broker who handled arrangements for her coffee shipment had called. Engine trouble had forced the container ship to make port in Belize for repairs. The shipment from Finca Velásquez would be delayed for a few days, maybe for as long as a week.

Chloe deleted the message with a philosophical shrug. Shipments were delayed from time to time. She would have liked Gerald Cox to see the warehouse stacked to the rafters, but it wouldn't be empty. Betancourt was not in immediate need of the coffee beans from Colombia—there were beans from Ecuador, Brazil, and Africa in the warehouse. And enough Colombian beans left from the last shipment to fill the immediate orders for the new Betancourt Estate Coffee brand.

No, the delay in the shipment was disappointing for another reason.

The telephone rang. Chloe picked up the receiver. "Hello?"

"Chloe, dear. I'm surprised you're not at the office, even if it is a gorgeous Saturday morning. All you ever do is work."

"Hi, Sylvie," Chloe said with a rueful sigh. Sylvie was right. All work and no play. "What about you? You work on Saturdays."

"True, the Sheridan Gallery is open on the weekend. But I take off during the week. You never do. What's wrong? You sound distracted. Is someone there with you?"

"No." Chloe paused. What had prompted Sylvie to think she wasn't alone? "Who would be here?"

"I thought perhaps your intriguing new secretary. How did last night go?"

"Extremely well. Zachary routed the Arcenaux boys as easy as pie. Thanks to him, I got to spend some quality time with Gerald Cox. He's coming to the office Monday for a tour, and to listen to my presentation."

"And did he have a tuxedo?"

"Oh, yes. He looked great."

"So that's not what's bothering you. What is it? Is all well with your precious coffee? Aren't you expecting shipment from Colombia soon?"

"Today, as a matter of fact, but there's a problem. The ship had engine trouble, so it won't be arriving for a few more days."

"I knew something was wrong. Your voice gives you away every time."

"I hope not. That wouldn't be very good for business."

"Don't worry. I only noticed because I'm a woman, and your friend. I think most men wouldn't hear the subtle nuances in your speech. For instance, a man wouldn't have heard the suppressed excitement when you spoke of your night with...what was his name? Your secretary?"

"Zachary Steele. What makes you think he excites me?"

"Doesn't he? I find him exciting. There's something very appealing about a shy, vulnerable man."

"Shy? Is that what he is?"

"Isn't he? Oh, my. Did the worm turn last night? Did he make a pass?"

"No, of course not." But *she* had. She'd *ordered* the man to kiss her. Guilt had her clearing her throat. She didn't think Sylvie could detect remembered lust in her voice, but she didn't want to take chances. "Really, Sylvie, he was a perfect gentleman."

"Then your problem is solved. You needed a man, and you've got one."

"For a few months." Suddenly, Chloe was not sure that was long enough. Something important had happened to her last night, and she hadn't had time to figure out exactly what that was.

"That should be an advantage—you never wanted a long-term relationship."

"That's right, I haven't."

"I never understood limiting oneself that way. I can see the advantages of one man at a time, but one man for a lifetime? I think not."

"So many men, so little time?" Chloe smiled.

"Exactly. And you must admit your assistant is nothing like your father. Although forceful men have their appeal, too."

"Not to me. Not at all. The last thing I want is another bully in my life."

"You have to get over your fear of men someday, Chloe. A nice, safe male like Zachary Steele is perfect for you."

"I don't want to take advantage of him." Frowning, Chloe gripped the receiver tighter. She *did* want to take advantage of Zachary. As soon as possible, and for as long as he was around.

"Chloe." Sylvie sounded exasperated. "For once, forget your scruples."

"I'm thinking about it." She'd already forgotten them. All except honesty. She would never lie to Zachary. He'd know exactly what she expected from their...liaison.

"Good for you. It's about time you discovered there are activities besides business in this world."

"Business pays the bills."

"So practical." Sylvie clucked. "Call your assistant, why don't you? Take him to—"

A bell chimed discreetly. Chloe recognized it as the bell over the door at Sylvie's art gallery. "Chloe, dear, a client has arrived. I'll talk to you later. Bye."

"Bye." Chloe hung up the receiver and sat on the bed.

Her father wasn't the only one who could make her feel inadequate. Sylvie, with her New York style and Bohemian experiences could leave her feeling gauche and unsophisticated. And scrupulous. But she should have called her on that one remark.

She wasn't *afraid* of men. Her father had exasperated and annoyed her, but he'd never given her any reason to fear him or any other man. Zachary, in particular, did not scare her. Hadn't she ordered him to kiss her? He hadn't wanted to, but she'd kissed him anyway. She'd been the aggressor, the one in control. If anyone had been terrorized in the back seat of that limo, it had been Zachary, not her.

Had she been too aggressive?

"Men like a woman who takes the lead. I'm sure I've heard that."

Some men, perhaps. Zachary obviously was not one of them. Unless Sylvie was right. Maybe shyness and not aversion had been what had kept Zachary from kissing her back. Could that be it? Or was she shamelessly using any old rationalization to justify her behavior?

Frowning, she crossed her arms across her chest. What about the way he'd behaved? Zachary had started the ball rolling—first, by volunteering to work overtime, then by claiming to be her fiancé. His part in setting up the limousine scene had not been exactly passive.

Chloe chewed on her bottom lip. Maybe she'd confused him. She had scolded him about his rash act, after all. She should have made it clear to him that she'd gotten over her pique before they got in the limo. In retrospect, Chloe could see that she'd been sending the poor man mixed signals.

She still wasn't completely sure what had made her decide she absolutely had to kiss Zachary last night. Her subconscious must have decided on an affair before she'd realized that was what she wanted. The seduction of Zachary Steele had begun with that kiss.

Chloe felt her face grow warm. She'd done more than kiss him—she'd climbed all over the man. "Oh, good grief. I sat on his injured leg!"

He hadn't said she hurt him. But Zachary was so diffident and self-effacing, he wouldn't have. He would have suffered in silence.

Is that what he'd been doing when she kissed him? Had he suffered the touch of her lips on his? Maybe. Maybe not. For a few seconds, before he'd pushed her off his lap, she'd gotten the impression that he was beginning to respond to her kiss.

But then he'd gotten huffy and said he wasn't that kind of man. Funny. She'd always assumed all men longed to be sex objects.

She had to face facts. Just because she found Zachary Steele attractive didn't mean the feeling was mutual. Darn. Here she had an opportunity for a perfect relationship, and the man was... What? Not interested?

Maybe she could arouse his interest.

She'd better be able to do that, or her career as a seductress would come to a screeching halt before it ever got started.

She had to spend more time with him at the office, and after hours. She needed to know more about him. If there was one thing she'd learned in her eight years as C.E.O. of Betancourt Coffees, knowledge was power. Chloe reached for the telephone on the nightstand. She'd call Zachary and invite him to brunch. Luckily, she'd thought to get his telephone number out of his personnel file before she'd left the office on Friday.

She dialed the number. Zachary didn't answer until the fifth ring.

"Zachary? Did I wake you?"

"No, Ms. Betancourt. I've been up for some time I went out for a walk. What can I do for you?"

"I thought we might meet for brunch. To discuss Mr. Cox's visit to the company on Monday. You need to tour the rest of the company's facilities, too. So you'll be able to answer his questions."

"Shouldn't you do that?"

"Oh, I will. Most of them. But, as my fiancé, you should know something about the business, too. And we'll have to decide what position you hold with the company."

"Trust me, Ms. Betancourt. I know my position. I'm your secretary." He sounded peeved.

"Yes, I know. But—"

"Are you ashamed of being engaged to a clerk?"

Not peeved. Upset. She had hurt his feelings. "No, of course not. Never mind about that. We'll just talk about—"

"I'm sorry. I shouldn't be so sensitive. You could tell Mr. Cox I'm your assistant and leave it at that."

"Thank you, Zachary. That's very considerate of you. Now about brunch." She glanced at the clock.

It was a little before ten. "Can you meet me at the Palace Café at eleven o'clock?"

"How about Café du Monde in twenty minutes? I'm not exactly dressed for a fancy restaurant."

"Well, then, Café du Monde it is. And make that thirty minutes. I just got out of the shower and I'm not dressed at all yet."

Chloe did a little dance as she hung up the telephone. She'd done it. She'd asked Zachary out, and he'd accepted. Now they would spend the whole day together. Surely by the evening she'd know if he'd be a willing partner in—

What? A flirtation? Another platonic relationship?

"I don't think so," she said out loud, searching her closet for the perfect thing to wear to breakfast with Zachary.

An affair. She, Chloe Betancourt, had decided she wanted an affair. No need to be coy about it—with herself, or with Zachary. This might be the only chance she'd ever have to find out about things like sex and passion. With a man who was willing, but one who followed her lead.

And her orders.

She had a very strong feeling that Zachary would cooperate if she handled him the right way. He'd just admitted he was sometimes overly sensitive, though. Keeping that in mind, she'd have to rein in her libido and practice a little subtlety.

Forty-five minutes later, Chloe slid into the chair Zachary held for her. "Sorry I'm late." She'd agonized too long over what to wear. After trying on everything in her closet, she'd ended up in jeans and a blue cashmere sweater. But the jeans were tight and the sweater clung to her curves. The gleam in Zachary's dark eyes as his gaze slid over her must mean he approved. "Have you been here long?"

"Long enough to decide I could handle an order of beignets. What would you like?"

"Café au lait and beignets. Thank you."

"I thought you drank your coffee black."

"Only if it's a Betancourt roast. Café du Monde is not one of our customers, unfortunately."

Zachary signaled the waiter and placed the order. A few minutes later the man returned to the table carrying a tray laden with coffee cups and plates of hot, square pastries liberally sprinkled with powdered sugar.

Between sugary bites, Chloe explained about the tour, and what Zachary needed to see before Monday. Dusting the powdery residue from her fingers, she changed the subject.

"Zachary, about our engagement..."

"Do you want to break it off?"

"No! I mean, do you?"

He shrugged. "Not unless you do. I realize I put you in an awkward position with Mr. Cox last night."

"You surprised me, that's all. But upon reflection, I think you came up with an excellent idea. Not only because of Mr. Cox and his bias in favor of family, but also because we...you and I..." Chloe cleared her throat. This part wasn't as easy as she'd thought it would be. "Last night in the limousine...perhaps I was too..."

"Eager?" Zachary actually grinned at her. Was he flirting?

"Aggressive?"

The grin faded away. "Perhaps. A little."

She reached across the table and took his hand in hers. "But you do understand that we have to appear to be...engaged."

Sweat broke out on Zachary's forehead, and he jerked his hand out from under hers. He seemed to be fighting some internal battle. "I suppose so."

Chloe tapped her fingers on the table. Talk about mixed signals. First he flirted, then he acted as if he couldn't stand her touch. "Really, Zachary. This was your idea."

"I didn't think it through."

"You didn't give either one of us time to think it through. But now we're in this relationship, and I, for one, think we should take full advantage of the opportunity to—"

"*Full* advantage?" Zachary wiped his forehead with a paper napkin.

"Yes. Our engagement really was a very clever idea, Zachary. I'm very pleased with you."

"Thank you, Ms. Betancourt."

"Chloe."

"Right. Chloe."

"Things might go smoother if we spent some time getting to know one another today. Before we have to face Mr. Cox on Monday morning. Tell me about yourself, Zachary. Where are you from?"

"The East Coast. Have you always lived in New Orleans?"

"Yes. My father's family has been here since before the Louisiana purchase. Mother's family came later, with the Americans."

"So Betancourt is a French name."

"Yes. Where on the East Coast?"

"North Carolina. The outer banks."

"I thought I detected a slight Southern drawl in your speech. I've never been to North Carolina. I haven't traveled much."

"Not even to where coffee beans grow?"

"Oh, yes. I've been to Brazil and Colombia. But only on business. Someday I'd like to travel for pleasure."

"Like your mother?"

"Yes. From her letters and postcards, I'd say she's a born tourist. She's having a wonderful time. About time, too. My father—never mind about him. Tell me more about you. How's your leg?"

"Better."

"Strong enough to walk to the warehouse from here?"

He glanced at his watch. "Not now. I have an appointment at noon."

"Oh? A luncheon date?"

"Not exactly." His eyes shifted away from hers.

Chloe had an awful thought. "Zachary, you aren't seeing anyone, are you? I mean, I wouldn't want our arrangement to interfere with any real involvement you might have."

"No. I don't have a girlfriend. My appointment is with a physical therapist."

"Oh! I didn't aggravate your condition when I—"

"When you sat on me? No."

"Oh, good." He was looking at her face again, his gaze not meeting her eyes. "Why are you looking at me like that?"

"You have powdered sugar on your nose." He reached over and brushed his fingertips across the bridge of her nose.

His touch made her nose tingle. She twitched it. "Is it gone?"

"You have a little on your upper lip." Grasping her chin, he used his thumb to rub it away.

More tingles, like spikes of electric energy. Chloe licked her lips. "Thank you, Zachary." Her voice was husky. "What about the tour? Will you have time later?"

"Sure. This should be a short session—it's the last one. I'll meet you at the office at two, all right?"

"Office? Oh, yes, the tour. Meet me there as soon as you're able to. I'll be waiting for you."

Zachary rose and held the chair for her as she stood. He really was a gentleman. As she turned, she found herself close to him. Close enough to see a trace of powdered sugar on his cheek. "Zachary? Bend down. You've got sugar on your cheek."

He tilted his head down, and Chloe boldly touched her mouth to his cheek, using her tongue to flick away the sugar.

A seductress had to start somewhere.

4

Rubbing his cheek, Zachary watched Chloe cross Canal Street, then he turned left and walked to the customs building. He had lied to Chloe. His appointment was not with a physical therapist—he'd seen the last of those people. His appointment was with his real employer.

He ought to tell the case agent he'd almost lost his objectivity. He ought to quit before he lost control and took Chloe up on her "practice" offer. Zach rubbed his eyes and shook his head to clear out the cobwebs. He wasn't thinking straight—not enough sleep. Every time he closed his eyes, his subconscious insisted on playing out the scene in the back of the limousine with sexy variations and erotic enhancements that should have made a grown man blush.

Zach never blushed.

And he never quit. There was no reason to withdraw from this assignment. His abrupt resignation from his position as Chloe's secretary would cause more problems than it would solve. So he had a problem keeping his hands off her. He could deal with it. How hard could it be to resist one little blond tyrant?

Glancing at the white pelican depicted in the stained-glass window over the entrance, Zach pushed open the heavy brass doors to the Custom House. He showed his identification to the guard, and walked up the marble stairs. The building was almost empty, but Bobby Williams, the baby-faced case agent, was waiting for him in the S.A.C.'s office on the second floor.

"The background check on Cox is under way, but no results are in yet. As it turns out, we've got time to follow up on him. The cargo ship with the container for Betancourt Coffees will be delayed for a few days. Engine trouble."

"Sabotage?"

"No reason to think so. I'm sure the smugglers are as disappointed as you are. You are disappointed, aren't you? This means you'll have to spend more time typing and filing." Bobby smirked at him.

"I can handle the office work," Zach told him through clenched teeth. And he could handle the overtime, too. He was a professional, after all.

"What are you going to do to pass the time?" Bobby asked.

"Check out the warehouse, for one thing. Ms. Betancourt is taking me on a tour this afternoon."

"How did you manage that?"

"Oh, didn't I tell you? Chloe and I are engaged."

"What?"

Zach quickly explained.

"Not bad, Steele. When you practice close surveillance, you really get close."

Zach rubbed his cheek again. Too damn close, if

he didn't do a better job of defending himself against Chloe's advances. "Yeah. Keep me posted on the progress of the coffee shipment. I want to be in the warehouse the night it arrives."

The case agent stood and slapped him on the shoulder. "Sure thing, big guy. Engaged, huh? That's got to be easier than getting shot at."

Zach nodded, although he could have argued the point. "I've got to get going. I'm meeting the target at two."

They shook hands, and Zach left the building. He walked swiftly down Magazine Street to Julia, then turned toward the river and South Peter Street, to the building that housed the offices of Betancourt Coffees.

He found Chloe in her office, with her day planner open to the next week. She looked up as he entered. "There you are. How did your session with the therapist go?"

"Good. I've got a clean bill of health."

She closed the calendar and stood. "Will you always limp?" she asked, her voice filled with sympathy.

"Maybe. But if I keep exercising, it should lessen in time."

She walked around the desk and squeezed his arm. "You *have* been working out. I can feel the muscles. I never noticed until last night. I suppose I was picturing you the way I first saw you."

He backed away. "That was a couple of weeks ago, at the job interview."

Chloe followed him. She placed her hands on his shoulders, then slowly trailed them down to his elbows and back. "Yes. And if you've been eating at Mother's, and working out, you'll be in great shape very soon. Not that you're in awful shape now. You really are a very attractive man, Zachary." She looked up at him and winked.

"Th-thank you, Ms. Betancourt."

"Oh, dear. You're blushing. I've embarrassed you."

"No. I never blush." Zach ignored the hot feeling on his face and jerked his arms free. "Where are we going first?"

"The warehouse. It's a couple of blocks from here. I thought we'd start there, then stop by the roasting room and the kitchens on the way back here. We'll take the same route on Monday when we show Mr. Cox around." Chloe returned to her desk, opened the top drawer, and took out a ring of keys. She took the day planner and the keys and stuffed them into a large shoulder bag. "I'm ready. Let's go."

"All the Betancourt buildings are within a few blocks?"

Chloe nodded. "My father planned to have all the facilities under one roof someday, but I don't see the need. We own the buildings, and nothing is too far away."

Zach held the door for Chloe. She tucked her arm through his. "We probably won't spend much time in the warehouse with Mr. Cox. I want him to see our test kitchen, and where we roast the coffee. Have you met the roast master?"

"Yes. He's come by the office a few times. How do the bags of coffee beans get from the ships to the warehouse?" Zach asked. He knew, but he wanted to keep Chloe occupied with something besides his attractiveness.

"By truck. Before the convention center was built, ships docked across the street from the warehouse, and we used forklifts to transfer the bags from the container ships. Now we have to transport the shipment from the Governor Nichols Street Wharf. Here we are."

She stopped in front of large sliding doors—doors big enough to admit a truck. A smaller door was cut into one of the large doors. It was padlocked. Chloe took the keys from her pocket, inserted one into the padlock on the small door and opened it.

No squeak, Zach noted. Someone took care to oil the hinges on a regular basis. "No one's here today? I thought a shipment was arriving from Colombia this afternoon."

"It's been delayed. It will be here later this week." Chloe stepped through the door and into the warehouse.

Zach followed. Bags of coffee beans were stacked on wooden pallets in seemingly haphazard fashion. Two forklifts were parked next to the open doors. The warehouse was not large. Finding a concealed spot from which to observe the smugglers could be a problem. "What's over there?" He pointed to a closed door in the far corner.

"A little office." Chloe walked over, her footsteps echoing on the concrete floor. She opened the door.

Zach looked over her shoulder into the interior of the small room. A scarred wooden desk held a telephone and a small television set. A counter, complete with sink, ran almost the width of the back wall. "Cozy," he said.

"No one uses it much, except for the night watchman. During the day people are in and out, taking beans from here to the roasting room next door. We roast every day. That's the advantage a small specialty company like Betancourt can give our customers—coffee roasted the same day it's delivered."

"Most of the customers are hotels and restaurants, right?"

"Yes. And hopefully, Cox's Coffee Emporiums."

"Why do you have a night watchman?"

"We've had a few attempted thefts over the years—usually when coffee prices skyrocket. Joe Jester is here from 10:00 p.m. to 6:00 a.m."

"Every night? Weekends included?"

"He has a replacement a couple of nights a week."

As they were leaving the office, Zach noticed three doors in the opposite wall. "More offices?" he asked.

"No. A couple of small storage rooms. The middle door leads to the alley, but no one uses it. The alley is too narrow for the trucks. Let's lock up here and get on with the tour."

For the remainder of the tour, Zach concentrated

on observing Chloe and listening to her explanations. She knew every facet of her business, he had to give her that. She also knew how to handle people. She demonstrated her executive ability by giving crisp, clear instructions and by judiciously bestowing praise when they were followed. Her employees reacted with pride and respect.

They'd seen everything by five. As they strolled back to the office, Zach thought about his surveillance problem. Where could he hide in the warehouse? One of the storerooms might work, he supposed. He'd check them out later. And what about the night watchman? How did the smugglers deal with him? Bribery? Chloe had mentioned prior attempted thefts, but no police reports had been filed after the two previous shipments from Finca Velásquez.

Maybe Chloe just gave the man the night off. Or maybe she told him there would be visitors. The point was, the night watchman wouldn't be a problem for her. She was his boss, after all.

"What are your plans for this evening?" Chloe asked, ending his speculations.

"Football. There's a playoff game on television tonight."

"Ah. You like sports."

"Sure. Don't you?"

"Oh, yes." She wound her arm through his and gave him a sultry look. "Especially the kind you play indoors. Would you like to come up for a cup of coffee?"

"I think I've had my quota for the day. After all

those samples you fed me at the test kitchen, I'm feeling a little wired." He tried to pull free, but she held on.

"Wine, then? It will help you relax."

"I'm more of a beer man than a wine drinker."

"Perfect. I've got beer—Abita Springs Wheat. Come on up."

"All right." Close surveillance, Zach reminded himself grimly.

Once in the apartment, Chloe insisted that he remove his jacket. She helped him take it off, sliding her hands down his arms as she did. She led him to the sofa and gave him a gentle push. "Sit right there. Put your feet up. I'll get the beer. It's in the refrigerator in the kitchen."

Zach leaned back and closed his eyes. How much was one man supposed to take? If Chloe touched him one more time, he wouldn't be responsible for his actions. His eyes popped open.

Of course, he would be. Responsible. Professional. True to his mission, like a good agent.

He should be looking around. Zach opened his eyes. There wasn't much to see that he hadn't seen the night before. The door she'd disappeared through had to lead to the kitchen, so the remaining door must lead to her bedroom. He'd like to take a peek, but he didn't want her to catch him snooping. She might get suspicious.

She might also get ideas. Look what she'd done in the back seat of the limo. In a bedroom, there was no telling what she might decide they needed to practice.

With a groan, Zach forced himself to concentrate on the facts. The dossier on Chloe included the information that Betancourt coffee beans arrived on a container ship from Colombia. Each container held two hundred-plus, sixty-kilo bags of beans, and Betancourt Coffees received one container from the *finca* every month to six weeks. As Chloe had verified, the bags of coffee beans were off-loaded at the Nichols Street wharf, then trucked to the Betancourt warehouse on South Peters Street.

The report had mentioned a night watchman, but had noted that the man was elderly, unarmed except for a nightstick, and prone to sleeping on the job.

"Or maybe he just follows orders," Zach muttered under his breath.

So far the facts established that Chloe had the knowledge, the opportunity, and the means to illegally import pre-Columbian artifacts. What could be her motive?

Money? Possibly, although if that were her motivation she hid it well. From what he'd seen, Chloe lived comfortably but not extravagantly. The dress she had worn Friday night had been flattering and attractive, but he didn't think it was a designer original. He made a mental note to have one of the female agents give him some input on the cost of Chloe's wardrobe.

Chloe hadn't been loaded down with diamonds or pearls, either. Her only jewelry had been tiny gold hoops in her pink, shell-like ears.

Zach cursed. Shell-like ears? Get a grip, Steele!

Grinding his teeth in frustration, he doggedly continued his analysis of Chloe's possible motivation.

Her legitimate income from Betancourt Coffees ought to be enough to support her life-style, unless she was one of those people who didn't know what enough was. Zach shook his head. Chloe didn't seem the greedy type.

If more money didn't ring her bell, could she be an adrenaline junky? Up until the limousine ride home, he would have said no. But his all-business little C.E.O. had shown him another side of her personality in the back seat of that limo.

Chloe Betancourt craved excitement.

Her old boyfriend—what was his name? Mark Michelet. She had said she missed him. Zach had relegated Mark to the role of convenient escort, the same relationship he had aspired to when he'd come up with the fiancé idea. Chloe had told the Sheridan woman she and Michelet had had a platonic relationship. But they must have been lovers. A woman like Chloe, full of hidden fire and passion—

Zach swore again. He'd never know about Chloe's appetite for passion. With luck, the investigation would end early Sunday morning with the smugglers caught red-handed. He'd return to Washington, and Chloe would spend the next few years in a federal penitentiary as a guest of Uncle Sam.

The thought of Chloe in prison stopped him in his tracks. His temporary boss thought she was one tough cookie, but she'd have a hard time dealing with life behind bars. A fierce need to protect Chloe from having to face the predators she'd surely meet there almost overwhelmed Zach's professional judgment. With a shake of his head, he made himself remember that what happened to Chloe was not his problem.

Unless she was innocent.

If he could prove that...

He had to get back to the warehouse that night. Chloe knew the shipment from Colombia was delayed. She would have no reason to return there tonight. But if other people were behind the smuggling, they might not be aware of the delay. It was unlikely that they had contact with anyone in the crew—the coffee beans from Colombia were not always shipped on the same container vessel, or even with the same shipping company.

Ergo, if anyone showed up at the warehouse tonight, Chloe would be in the clear.

"Here's the beer. Sorry I took so long." Chloe entered the living room carrying a tray.

Zach stood and took the tray from her. She'd brought two bottles of beer, two frosted mugs and an assortment of snacks—pretzels, beer nuts, several kinds of cheese. She'd also left something behind. Her bra.

"You didn't have to go to all this trouble."

"Yes, I did. Put the tray on the coffee table and sit down, Zachary." She patted the cushion next to her.

He pretended not to notice, heading for the wing chair opposite the love seat.

"Not way over there. Come sit by me. This may take a while."

"What may take a while?"

"Things. The wrap-up of our tour, for starters. Do you have any questions about the coffee business?"

"No. You covered everything very clearly."

"Thank you. All right, that part's taken care of. But we have more work to do if we're going to convince Mr. Cox that we're engaged."

"Work?"

"You're right, Zachary. We shouldn't look on this as work. This should be more like play, for both of us."

"Play?" He couldn't keep his gaze from dropping to her chest. She'd definitely taken off her bra, the hussy. And she had bedroom games on her mind, he'd bet his badge on it. He had to get out of range, or risk compromising more than the investigation. "What do you mean?"

"I'm talking about our behavior."

He eyed her warily. "What about it?"

"Now that Mr. Cox knows we're...intimate, he'll expect us to behave like lovers."

"In public?"

"Yes." She scooted closer, pressing her hip against his.

"I don't think so."

"Yes, Zachary. You have to stop that."

"Stop what?"

"You get twitchy every time I get close to you."

"Twitchy?"

"Twitchy. And you blush."

"I do not twitch!" Zach wanted to deny blushing, but he couldn't, not when his face felt hot.

"You do. You're doing it now." She tucked her hand through his arm. "I can feel it. When I touch you, you get noticeably nervous. That won't do. I think, if you're really feeling all right, that we should practice."

"Oh, Lord."

"Zachary? You cannot jerk away every time I touch you. Mr. Cox will wonder what's going on. If we spend more time together, I'm sure we can find a way to get through this comfortably. We might even have fun."

"Fun?"

"Fun. I find you very attractive, Zachary. I like the idea of touching you, kissing you." She leaned against him. "Don't you want to try, at least?"

Swallowing a groan, Zach said, "I guess I owe you that much. I did get us engaged."

Chloe beamed her hundred-watt smile at him. "Yes, you did. I'm so glad you see it my way."

"All right, we can practice. Touching. Would you like to dance?"

Chloe pulled away from him. She looked incredulous. "Dance? You want to dance?"

"Yes. That involves touching."

"That's not exactly the kind of touching I had in mind."

"That's the only kind of touching I feel comfortable with. The other kind—well, we could go too far."

"How far is that?"

"I'll know when we get there."

"How about this? I promise I will stop whenever you say stop."

Yeah, right. If he fell for that line, next she'd be selling him a prime piece of swampland. "I want to dance." Zach wanted to take charge of this little experiment. How would Chloe react if he grabbed her and kissed her silly? He didn't dare risk it. He had to keep his head.

The blue sweater molded to Chloe's breasts, which were close enough to touch. His fingers itched to find out. She leaned closer. "Touch me, Zachary."

"Where?"

"Anywhere. Anywhere at all."

He put a hand on her denim-covered knee. It seemed like the safest place. Squeezing gently, he looked at her.

She was frowning. "You can do better than that. Take me in your arms."

"Only if we're standing up. Let's dance."

"Oh, all right." Chloe stood and walked to the stereo. She chose a CD, and the room filled with the sound of music.

Slow-dancing music. Zach gulped. Maybe dancing hadn't been such a good idea, after all. A few erotic moves of Chloe's hips and he would be a goner.

Chloe returned to the love seat, and held out her hand. "Shall we dance, Mr. Steele?"

Zach stood and took her in his arms.

"Hold me closer." She pressed closer, flattening her soft breasts against his chest.

A surge of testosterone had Zach's arms tightening around her.

"That's more like it." Chloe purred the words against his neck. She tangled her fingers in his hair and pulled his head down. "Now let's try a kiss."

"While we're dancing?"

"People kiss when they dance."

Zach brushed his mouth on hers.

"Harder," she ordered, moving sensuously against his thighs.

He pushed her away. "Stop. That's enough."

"So soon? We barely got started."

"I'm thirsty." He sat on the love seat. Reaching for one of the open beer bottles, he drank deeply. When he lowered the bottle, he found himself staring into Chloe's big, blue eyes.

She looked disgruntled. And determined. "Are you finished?"

"Yeah. I should go."

"Not yet."

He replaced the bottle on the tray. "I really should go."

"Zachary, we haven't practiced nearly enough." She sat next to him.

"I think we have. I didn't twitch, did I?"

"You did, too. And that kiss was pitiful."

"Pitiful?" Zach lost his tenuous hold on his control. He grabbed Chloe by the shoulders and pushed her deep into the cushions, letting her feel his weight.

He found her mouth with his. With his lips parted, and his tongue tangling with hers, he kissed Chloe hot and hard, making it last until they were clinging to one another, gasping for breath.

When he finally managed to lift his head, Chloe's blue eyes were staring at him again. They were filled with wonder, filling him with pure masculine satisfaction.

"Wow! That was...wow." She smiled at him.

"Yeah, it was." Guilt replaced the smug pleasure he'd felt. He'd gotten caught up in Chloe's fantasy, and he'd almost let her take things too far. Abruptly, he sat up, bringing her with him.

"No twitches," she said, grinning at him.

"Not one." He tried putting some space between them.

Chloe twisted in his arms, snuggling closer. "More," she ordered, sounding breathless.

"Much more and we'll have to make this engagement the real thing."

She took his face in her hands. "No, we won't. Let me make this very clear, Zachary. I am not interested in marriage. Only in...more."

"I don't think more is a good idea, Chloe. Not now."

"Now is the perfect time for more. We're here, we're alone. And I'm—"

The telephone rang.

"Where's the phone?"

"Doesn't matter. I'm not going to answer it," she said, tugging at his shirt. "Let the machine pick up."

He grabbed her hands. "Listen. It might be important."

After Chloe's recorded announcement, a masculine voice came on the line. "Ms. Betancourt. Gerald Cox here. I'm calling to cancel our meeting on Monday. I've got to return to Florida, but I'll be back in a week or so. Call my office in Pensacola and we'll set up another time for the tour." He rattled off a number.

Zach let Chloe go and reached for his beer. He tilted the bottle and drained it in two swallows. "If Cox isn't going to be around, we can put off more practice for now."

She looked confused. "Practice? That was practice?"

"Isn't that what we were doing?"

"Yes, but—"

"But what? We've done enough, Chloe. I won't jerk away when you touch me anymore."

"I should hope not."

"And I'm sure I'll be able to dance with you and kiss you in public without blushing."

She straightened her sweater. "I have no doubt. But, Zachary—"

"Stop." He held his hands up, palms out, interrupting her. "I've got to go, Chloe. That game I planned to watch tonight is starting in a few minutes. Thanks for the beer."

Zach almost tripped over his own feet in his hurry to get away. Once he'd closed the apartment door behind him, he breathed a sigh of relief. His exit might have been awkward, cowardly even, but he'd done the right thing. There were some lines a man could not cross. Letting himself be seduced by Chloe was one of them.

When he reached the street, Zach hesitated. He could go home and try to get some sleep. Yeah, right. Like his hormone-loaded body was going to relax anytime soon.

He headed for the warehouse instead. Time to use some of his undercover skills on the night watchman. He'd come up with some story about why he was out and about late on a Saturday night, then see if he could worm some useful information out of the man.

5

Zach arrived at the office early Monday morning. He hadn't seen or heard from Chloe since Saturday night, when he'd managed to escape her apartment with his honor tattered but intact.

As planned, he had spent the rest of Saturday night at the warehouse, drinking coffee and playing checkers with Joe Jester, the night watchman. Jester had let him in once Zach showed him his Betancourt Coffees employee ID. He'd told Joe that he'd been working late, and that he thought he'd stop by and introduce himself to a fellow nightshift employee on his way home.

Zach hadn't gotten much for his trouble. Joe might have been bored, but he wasn't much of a talker. He'd answered Zach's cautious queries about his job with monosyllables. But the man had gotten even more tight-lipped when Zach had asked him if he'd ever seen any action on the job. Whether his obvious guilt feelings stemmed from criminal participation or only neglect of duty, Zach could not tell. But before he left, Zach had managed to lay the groundwork for a return visit whenever the shipment from Colombia arrived. He'd told Joe that he suffered from insomnia, and that playing checkers was as good a way as any to pass the sleepless hours.

Zach had slept most of Sunday, grateful that Chloe hadn't called with another excuse to continue with her lessons on how engaged couples behaved. His subconscious had taken over the teaching chore, as it turned out. He had dreamed about her again. The details were a little fuzzy, but he remembered the tone of the dream—less lusty, more romantic.

Zach was not a romantic.

Never had been. He would admit to having been somewhat idealistic in his younger days. When he'd been recruited by customs, the idea of wearing a badge and catching bad guys had proved an irresistible lure. Still did, for that matter. But just because a man believed in honor, truth, and justice didn't mean he was an idiot where women were concerned. He hadn't met the female who could make him buy roses or eat dinner by candlelight. Especially not a female target. That wouldn't be romantic. That would be stupid.

Taking his place behind the secretarial desk, Zach began sorting through the morning mail.

Chloe walked in just as he opened the last envelope. She looked as tired this morning as he'd felt after his long Saturday night. Zach half rose from his chair. He wanted to take her in his arms and hold her, tell her everything would be all right. Stupid. Gritting his teeth, he stayed in his chair, but he couldn't completely ignore her bedraggled appearance. "Is anything wrong?"

"Nothing," said Chloe.

"Are you sure? You look—"

"Like something the cat dragged in. I know. It's lucky Mr. Cox canceled the tour this morning. I don't feel up to making a dynamic presentation this morning." Pausing to pick up her mail, Chloe said, "Hold my calls, will you? As long as I have the morning free, I've got some personal things to take care of."

Chloe closed the door to her office. Zach sat at the desk and waited. He wanted to barge in after her and demand that she tell him what was going on. She hadn't even made a pass at him this morning. He ought to be relieved, but he felt disgruntled.

And disappointed.

Zach spent the morning answering the telephone and composing replies to the letters Chloe had left for him to handle. In between chores, he tried to figure out when he'd gotten soft in the head. He was finding it more and more difficult to remain objective. He wanted to believe that Chloe could not be involved in any kind of criminal activity. He still had enough brain cells functioning to realize that his doubts about her guilt could be nothing more than wishful thinking.

If Chloe were innocent, she would no longer be a target. Then he could tell her who he was and concentrate on his own personal investigation of the emotions she inspired in him.

The telephone rang, interrupting his self-analysis.

Sylvie Sheridan, the most persistent caller that

morning, said, "I really must insist that you let me talk to Chloe," she said. "This is the third time you've put me off."

"I'm sorry, Ms. Sheridan. Miss Betancourt left strict instructions that she was not to be disturbed."

"Do you have any idea what she's doing?"

"No." Using the wiretap, Zach had heard her make several calls, to a florist, a baker, and a minister. It sounded to him as if she were planning a wedding. Whose, he hadn't a clue. The thought had crossed his mind that she might be trying to make their fake engagement look real. But with Cox out of the picture temporarily, that didn't wash.

"I'm coming over there. Right now." Sylvie practically snarled the words.

"That's up to you, but she may not see you."

"She'll see me. I'm her best friend."

Zach winced as Sylvie slammed the receiver down. "So long, friend," he muttered. What did Chloe see in the woman? They had little in common as far as he could see. True, they were both entrepreneurs, but in very different kinds of businesses. Chloe owned a coffee company. Sheridan owned an...art gallery.

Leaning back in his chair, Zach's eyes narrowed. He really had gotten soft in the head. He should have seen it sooner. Sylvie Sheridan, art gallery owner. She would have connections in the art world, possibly to the shadowy places where wealthy collectors paid outrageous prices for stolen works of art. Sylvie could be using Chloe's business as a means of importing her merchandise. Without Chloe's knowledge.

Or Sylvie and Chloe could be working together.

The outer door opened and Sylvie swept past him. "She *will* see me." She entered Chloe's office without knocking.

Zach picked up the earphones for the Dictaphone. This was one conversation he wanted very much to hear.

"Chloe, what is the matter?"

"Nothing." There was a pause, then she added, "Everything. It's Mother." Zach could hear the strain in her voice.

"Your mother. What's wrong with her? Is she ill?"

"Worse. She's in love."

Zach heard Sylvie's throaty chuckle. "I'm sorry, I don't see the problem."

"She called me late last night. That's the first time she's done that—usually she calls me in the morning. For weeks, Mother has been telling me about the man, but I never thought—"

"Who is he? A foreigner? A fortune hunter?"

"No, he's a professor from U.N.O., one of the tour lecturers. She thinks he's wonderful."

"And?"

"And he proposed to her yesterday, and she accepted. She sounds so happy." The wiretap picked up Chloe's deep sigh. "I should be happy for her."

"Yes. You will be, as soon as you get used to the idea. There are advantages for you."

"What advantages?"

"You won't have to support her any longer."

"I don't support her." From her tone, Zach could almost see Chloe bristling with indignation.

"You run the business. She gets her income from Betancourt Coffees, doesn't she?"

"Yes, but she owns half the business."

"And you do all the work."

"I love the work," Chloe said emphatically. Her voice softened. "And Mother loves Professor John Anderson. She's going to marry him on Christmas Day."

"I don't suppose you'll be able to attend the wedding. You couldn't traipse off to Europe, could you? What would happen to your business? Who would schedule the coffee shipments?"

"That's not a problem. They're getting married here. At home. Mother gave me a list of things to do before they arrive. I have to decorate the house for Christmas, and get things arranged for the wedding. Florist, bakery, invitations, that kind of thing. It was interesting, the way she was snapping orders like... like Dad used to do."

"That's all right, then." Zach thought Sylvie sounded more relieved than the news warranted—unless she was afraid to lose her source of information about shipments from Colombia. "She can't be planning a large wedding, not on such short notice."

"She's not. Only a few friends—that means you, for one—and family. It's that she's getting *married!* She was just getting to the point where she was comfortable doing things for herself, and now she's going to be a wife again."

"And that means?"

"What if she reverts? Lets him order her around, make all the decisions. You know."

"No, I don't."

"Of course, you don't. You're a strong woman, Sylvie. But Mother...isn't. Wasn't. I thought she was getting stronger, but now...."

"If she's not so strong, then a man to take care of her is just what she needs."

"I suppose so. I do want her to be happy. I know she's been lonely ever since Dad died." There was a pause. Zach thought he heard a sniffle. Chloe wasn't crying, was she? He couldn't stand it if she were crying. "I didn't spend enough time with her."

"What time? You never had time for yourself. You could take a lesson from your mother. Take a vacation. See the world. Find a man. Or two, or three."

"One is more than enough."

"That one being your secretary, I presume. How are things progressing?"

"Slowly. Sylvie, it was nice of you to drop by, but I really have a lot to do today, so—"

"Oh, my. I forgot. Isn't today the day you are to meet with...the coffee shop man? What is his name?"

"Cox. Gerald Cox. I was, but he postponed the tour."

"And your precious cargo? Any word on the shipment?"

"Not yet. I'll check with the shipping agent later today."

"Well, then, now that I see you are in control, as usual, I'll leave you to it."

Zach dropped the earphones just as Sylvie exited Chloe's office. Chloe followed her and walked with her to the door. As soon as Sylvie had left, Chloe took her coat from the closet. "I'm going home."

"You'll be at your apartment for the rest of the day?"

"No. Sorry. I guess I still think of my parents' house as home. I'm going there. My mother wants me to see to the Christmas decorations."

"She'll be home for Christmas?"

"A week or so before. Long enough to get a blood test and a marriage license."

"She's getting married?"

"So it would seem."

"You're not happy about it."

"I'm trying to be. I will be, as soon as I've had time to get used to the idea." She smiled, but the smile quivered some.

"Don't you approve of the man?"

"It's not the man. The man is wonderful, if half of what my mother says about him is true. It's the institution. I'm not a fan of marriage."

Zach thought of his parents, a crusty New England sea captain married to a Southern belle. He'd grown up watching them fall more in love every day—and that included the days when they weren't speaking as well as the days when they communicated by yelling at each other. "Some people seem to make it work."

"Yes, when the women people do everything the men people tell them to do."

"Do you need any help?" Stifling the nostalgic memories of his childhood, Zach reminded himself that searching the Betancourt family residence had been on his list of things a good undercover agent should do.

She paused, long enough for Zach to wonder if she was going to turn down his offer. "I could use some help," she said finally. "Jeannine can answer the telephone for a few hours."

"I'll forward the calls to her office." Zach did not want anyone else fooling around with the Dictaphone. He dialed the office down the hall where the bookkeeper worked and told Jeannine he and Chloe would be out of the office for a few hours. "Shall I call a taxi?"

"No, let's take the streetcar. Mother's house is on State Street, a few houses from St. Charles Avenue."

After a short streetcar ride, Chloe led the way to a Victorian house surrounded by a wrought-iron fence. She unlocked the gate and they walked up the brick pathway to the porch.

"This is where you grew up?" Zach looked at the two-story house, colorfully painted pale peach with lavender gingerbread and dark green shutters. A round turret room on one end of the porch soared three stories high.

Chloe smiled. "It's a nice house, isn't it?" She

opened the door and led Zach into a wide hallway. A stairway curved gracefully up to the second floor.

"Very nice." Zach looked around. The house was warm and inviting, and it looked lived in. "How long has your mother been gone?"

"Several months. She left right after Labor Day." Her chin trembled. Chloe sat down on the stairs and rested her chin on her hands. "I never should have moved out. But as long as I stayed at home, Mother expected me to tell her what to do, and when. I didn't want to turn into Dad."

Zach sat down next to her. "You didn't like your father."

"I didn't like the way he treated my mother."

"Did he abuse her?"

She looked shocked. "No. The opposite. He spoiled her rotten. Gave her everything she wanted—this house, charge accounts at all the stores, fabulous vacation trips twice a year."

"I see. A real brute."

Chloe smiled. "That doesn't sound so bad, does it? You're right. Dad was not a brute, but he was domineering. He treated Mother like a child, and a not-too-bright child at that. He made all the decisions. He told Mother who to entertain and when, what clubs to join, what charities to volunteer for. He didn't even let her have her own checking account. He gave her the credit cards, and he paid the bills, but she didn't have a clue how to take care of herself, much less a business, when he died."

"That's why you stepped in and took over the coffee company?"

"I had to. Not that I was any better prepared than she was. I majored in French literature, for heaven's sake. Daddy didn't think his little girl needed to know anything practical. After all, some man was going to marry me and take care of me for the rest of my life."

"And you can take care of yourself."

"Darn right."

"But your mother can't."

"I'm not sure. She's learned a lot since Dad died, but I'm afraid...if the man she's met is like most men, he'll expect to be in charge, and she'll let him take over. She's never been comfortable looking out for herself. I think she may want a man to..."

"Guide and protect her?"

"Is that what you call bossing her around?"

"Did she object to it?"

"No. She didn't. But I did. Dad had expectations for me, too. He wanted me to be like her."

"And you wanted to be like him."

"I did not."

"You don't want to be boss? The one in charge?"

"Oh." Chloe's eyes widened. "I never thought of it that way."

Zach could see it—Chloe and her father nose to nose. Too bad the man had died young. They might have reached an accommodation, in time. One that would allow Chloe to admit that needing a man was not always a bad thing. Not when the man needed the woman just as much. He ran a finger along the banister. "No dust."

"Mother arranged for a cleaning service before she left."

"She let strangers into her house when no one was here?"

"It's a reputable firm. And there isn't anything that valuable here anyway."

"No jewelry? No furs?"

"Mother took her good jewelry with her. No furs. Who needs fur in New Orleans? It's November, and the temperature is still in the sixties most days."

"No Renoirs? No Monets?"

"No. I told you, we got rid of Dad's art collection. But it never ran to old masters."

"Renoir and Monet aren't old masters—they're Impressionists."

"Oh. I should know things like that—Sylvie has lectured me often enough. How is it you know so much about art?"

"I took a few courses in art history in college."

"So did I, but it didn't stay with me." Taking his hand, Chloe stood up, pulling him with her. "Anyway, let's get on with the business at hand. First, I want to get Mother's Christmas folder. That will be in the study." Chloe opened a door off the wide central hallway. A desk sat in front of a bay window overlooking the street, and a wooden file cabinet stood next to it. "Check the file cabinet for a folder marked Christmas, will you? I'm going to turn up the thermostat. It's chilly in here."

Zach opened the file cabinet and found the folder Chloe wanted. He quickly flipped through the other folders, his fingers stopping at a folder marked Pre-Columbian Artifacts. Heart racing, he pulled both folders out, and deliberately dropped them on the floor. Papers scattered across the Persian rug.

Chloe returned from the hallway as he was kneeling to retrieve them. "Oh, my, what happened?"

"I dropped a couple of folders. Clumsy. I'll put everything back in order." As he picked up each piece of paper, he scanned it quickly. The items from the pre-Columbian folder were letters. From museum curators, government officials, and the like. Each thanked Señora Claudia Betancourt and Señorita Chloe Betancourt for returning an artifact to its country of origin. "What are these?" he asked.

"What? Oh, the letters we got when we gave Dad's pre-Columbian collection away."

"Why did you do that? Wasn't it worth a lot of money?"

"Some of the pieces were, I suppose. At first, Mother wanted to donate the collection to N.O.M.A.—the New Orleans Museum of Art. She was on the board at the time. It was actually the curator's idea for us to return the pieces to South America. He told us about the laws that prevent the export of such items from those countries now. Mother and I talked it over, and we decided to do it. Sylvie took care of it for us."

"Did she?" While Chloe was sorting through the papers, Zach managed to stuff two of the letters into his inside jacket pocket. Things were looking better and better for Chloe. And worse for Sylvie. She was the one who had brought up the shipment from Colombia. Why? Concern for her friend? Not likely. She hadn't been that concerned about Chloe's problem with her mother's hasty wedding plans. She hadn't offered to help, he'd noticed. But she had asked about the shipment of coffee beans from Colombia. Chloe's business supplies should concern Sylvie even less than Mrs. Betancourt's marriage—unless she had something arriving on the same boat.

"You're frowning. What's wrong?"

"Not a thing. I was woolgathering." His gut feeling had been right—Chloe was not a criminal.

"What about? Now you're grinning like an idiot."

"Christmases past. What's in the Christmas folder?"

"Mother keeps records of everything. How many poinsettias she used to decorate the porch and the stairway, where she got them, how much she paid for them. She also has information on trees, garland, wreaths, and so on."

"Sounds like your mother is a very organized woman."

"She is—as long as it has to do with running a household or a charity ball."

"A natural-born homemaker?"

"I don't know if she was born to the role, or if my father trained her for it. Mother was only eighteen when they got married. Let's get the ornaments down, and then go buy a tree. Trimming the tree is my favorite Christmas activity."

Chloe's eyes were sparkling like sapphires again. She'd apparently recovered from the shock of her mother's wedding announcement. "I take it you like Christmas?"

"I love all the holidays. New Year's Eve, the Fourth of July, Mardi Gras. Parades and fireworks make a holiday special, don't you think?"

"Yeah. I like fireworks, too."

"Most of all, I love Christmas. Of course, I liked it more back in the days when a party was a party, and not a business affair. Come on, the attic is this way." Chloe led the way upstairs. Another wide hallway had four doors opening off it, two on each side. Bedrooms, he supposed.

Chloe pointed to the ceiling, and Zach pulled down the folding ladder. She scrambled up. He followed more slowly, enjoying the view of her long legs and shapely rear.

Chloe flicked a light switch and sneezed. "It's dusty up here."

"Attics are supposed to be dusty. And cobwebby." Zach looked around. "No cobwebs."

"Good. I don't like spiders. The decorations are over there." She pointed to three large boxes in the corner.

"Quite a collection."

"Some of the ornaments belonged to my great-grandmother, and we add more every year. At least one or two. I'm sure Mother is bringing at least one from every country she's visited this fall. Luckily the house has twelve-foot ceilings on the first floor. We can get a tree tall enough to hold all of them."

"There's a Christmas tree lot close to my apartment building. I pass it on the way to work."

"There's one closer, a few blocks over on Prytania. We'll walk over there as soon as we get the decorations down. You're sure you don't mind helping with all this? We'll need garland, too, to decorate the banister and to drape over the doorways. Poinsettias, lots of them, for the front porch. We can get those at the florist shop on St. Charles. I need to talk to them about the flowers for the wedding, anyway. And lights. The little white kind, for the shrubbery. Those should be in one of the boxes."

"How many days until Christmas?"

"Enough. I hope. We can do it. Once we've got everything organized, it should only take a day or two to decorate the house. Then I can concentrate on the wedding preparations."

Zach carried the boxes down from the attic one by one, as Chloe hovered. "I'm not going to drop them."

"I know." She opened the boxes and located the Christmas lights. "What kind of Christmas traditions does your family have?"

Zach took a strand from her and began untangling it. "Hmm, let's see. Mom serves her famous fish stew on Christmas Eve. After dinner, everyone gets to open one package, but the rest have to wait until morning. First one up—that's usually my father—has to fix breakfast. Then the three of us open an obscene number of packages—"

"Three? What about your sister?"

"Sis—oh, her. She and her family live on the coast."

"Which one?"

"Uh. West. Far away. We hardly ever see her anymore."

"That's too bad. Don't you hate it when families get so spread apart? My mother's sisters both married men from other places. Aunt Lou is in San Antonio, and Aunt Kathleen is in Little Rock. I'm sure they'll both make it home for the wedding, though, along with my uncles and cousins." She beamed at him. "A family reunion for Christmas. This will be fun! I don't know why I was so upset this morning. Are you planning on going home for Christmas this year?"

"I'm not sure."

"You need to go home. Your parents shouldn't have to spend the holidays alone. Don't worry about time off. You've worked enough overtime to make up for any days you need to take to get home. And you'd better make reservations right away. The flights may already be full."

"I'll call home and see what the plans are. Sis and her family may be making the trek this year. Or Mom and Pop may be planning a trip somewhere. They do that sometimes. Last year they went to Williamsburg."

"Your parents live in North Carolina?"

"Yes. Most of the time. They have a cottage in

Maine, where Pop's from originally. They spend the summers there, sometimes. Business permitting."

"What does your father do?"

"He runs a fleet of charter boats out of Elizabeth City."

"And you're working as a secretary?"

"I get seasick." He set the last box on the floor at the foot of the stairs.

"Did your father think...less of you because you couldn't follow in his footsteps?"

Zach shot her a startled look. "Why would you think that?"

"A sea captain and a boy who..."

"Threw up every time the boat rocked?" Pasting a mournful look on his face, Zach nodded. "You're very perceptive."

"It must have been hard for you...a sensitive, gentle young boy growing up with a man like that."

"It took a while for us to reach an understanding." Their agreement being that Zach would stay the hell away from the boats. He'd been the one determined to overcome what he'd thought of as a weakness. His father had been more sanguine. His mother had joined her considerable influence to his when Zach had almost died of dehydration after spending several days at sea with one of his father's competitors. That had ended his days at sea once and for all.

"Your father wasn't cruel to you?"

"No. He teased me about my weakness, of course."

"He called you a coward?"

"Is that what you think I am?"

"No. Not at all. I think you're a gentle, sweet man."

"Really? Sweet?"

"As sugar, remember?" She grinned at him.

He was beginning to feel a little insulted. Chloe thought he was a coward, did she? She probably thought he'd been an art major. The truth was, he'd taken the art history courses to get close to a pretty classmate. He'd gotten his degree in criminal justice, but the art courses had come in handy. He'd been recruited by customs after he'd exposed a forgery ring led by one of his professors.

Zach was not a sissy.

As soon as he finished this investigation, he'd take great pleasure in showing Chloe a thing or two about "sweet" men. "Now what?"

"Now we look for the perfect Christmas tree." Chloe eyed him, forgetting about her own problems long enough to notice Zachary was very forthcoming about some aspects of his family, and almost secretive about others. What could have happened between him and his sister? He acted almost as if he'd forgotten about her. And his relationship with his father must have been as turbulent as hers had been with her dad. They really had a lot in common.

As they walked side by side to the Christmas tree lot, Chloe talked about her Christmases past. "We always eat out on Christmas Eve—at Commander's Palace or Antoine's or Galatoire's, some place special. Restaurants in New Orleans have special Christmas menus. Then we go to midnight mass and afterward, back at home, we turn off all the lights except for the ones on the Christmas tree. We light a fire in the fireplace, and toast Christmas with eggnog or hot chocolate."

"A fire? Every year?"

"Yes." She grinned at him. "Of course, some years we have to turn the air-conditioning down really low."

Zachary laughed.

The laughter continued as they argued playfully over which tree was absolutely perfect, which branch had to have another ornament, and whether tinsel should be hung one strand at a time, or tossed on in clumps. But at last the tree was decorated. Chloe turned on the lights.

"It's beautiful," she breathed, staring at the tree.

"Beautiful," Zachary agreed, looking at her. "What next?"

"That's enough for today. Look at the time—it's after five and it's dark outside."

"When will the poinsettias arrive? Did the florist say?" Chloe had called and placed an order during a break in decorating the tree.

"Later this week."

"What about the wreath?"

"Same time. I forgot something."

"What?"

She advanced on him. "Mistletoe."

Zachary stood his ground. "So we did. I think I

saw some growing on the oak tree in front of the house."

"There usually is. We always hang a bunch right there." She pointed to the archway over his head.

"Do you want me to get some for you?"

"Later. For now, use your imagination." Chloe stepped closer, and wound her arms around Zachary's neck. Gently, she pulled his head down until she could touch her mouth to his. Only a feathery kiss at first—she didn't want to scare him.

They'd had so much fun today, decorating the tree, exchanging stories of their childhood Christmas memories. She had to go slow, or risk spoiling their new camaraderie. On the other hand, she wanted him to know she wanted him.

She needed to find out if he wanted her.

She kissed him again, this time parting her lips ever so slightly.

With a groan, Zach surrendered. His hands went to her tiny waist and pulled her tightly against him. Accepting the invitation of her softly parted lips, he thrust his tongue into her waiting sweetness. He might hate himself in the morning, but he had to have another taste of her.

Chloe couldn't help the tremors shaking her from head to toe. Exultant, she pressed herself closer to Zachary and deepened the kiss. He did want her.

"That's enough," he said.

She stuck her lower lip out. "You always say that. When won't it be enough?"

"Better not pout, Chloe," Zach said, sidestepping her question. "Santa won't bring you anything."

Reluctantly, Chloe let him go. She was much too old to write a letter to Santa Claus. But if she weren't, she knew exactly what she'd ask him to stuff in her Christmas stocking—Zachary Steele.

6

The next morning, Zach took the letters he'd pilfered from Mrs. Betancourt's file cabinet to Custom House and gave them to the case agent. He asked that they be verified, and that a background investigation be done on Sylvie Sheridan.

"She owns a gallery. According to Chloe, she's the one who handled the return of her father's collection to South America."

"Think she's working with Betancourt?" Bobby Williams asked.

"Maybe. Or maybe she's working alone. I've overheard several of their conversations, and they have never discussed the smuggling business."

"So? They may suspect the place is wired."

"I don't think so. I think Chloe may not be involved at all."

"You're not taking this fiancé business too far, are you? Getting involved with a suspect would not be a good career move."

"I know that," Zach said, guilt making him curt. "It just doesn't make sense that Chloe would give away artwork worth thousands of dollars just so she could steal it, or stuff like it, back again."

"I'll have the letters checked. The Sheridan woman, too."

Zach looked at his watch. "Call me as soon as you have anything. I've got to hustle or I'll be late for work."

He arrived a few minutes after nine o'clock. Chloe was waiting for him, but she didn't comment on his tardiness. "We've got to plan our week." She held up a stack of envelopes. "I've got invitations galore to go through."

After looking through them, Chloe decided on a luncheon on Wednesday, a cocktail party Thursday night, and a dinner party on Friday. "The luncheon involves a fashion show. Not many men attend those." She tapped the invitation against her chin, and looked at him pensively. "You do need some time to yourself, I suppose. For Christmas shopping. Have you decided whether or not you're going home for the holidays?"

"Not yet."

"Well, I don't really need an escort for the luncheon. I'll see if Sylvie wants to go."

The telephone rang. "I'll get it." Zach answered the phone, "Betancourt Coffees," then handed her the receiver. "It's the shipping broker."

Chloe took the receiver from him, her fingers brushing his. "Hello. What's up?" She listened for a few minutes, then hung up the telephone. "The Velásquez shipment is arriving Friday afternoon."

Zach frowned. He could hope the dinner party would be over early, but he knew better. New Orleanians treated dining as an art form, and no dinner worth its cayenne pepper would end before ten or eleven o'clock. How could he get out of escorting Chloe on Friday night?

"Zachary?"

"Yes, sorry. Did you say something?"

"I said forget about Friday night. I've changed my mind about that invitation. The Delacroixs always have a brunch on New Year's Day. I'll touch base with them then."

She looked as innocent as a baby, but why would *she* cancel dinner Friday night? Did she plan to be at the warehouse? Zach hoped not. He was ninety-nine percent sure Chloe was not involved in the smuggling, but that last one percent was proving illusive.

The percentage of uncertainty jumped a few points later in the week when Bobby Williams called him with a report.

"The letters are forgeries. Not one of the items from Charles Betancourt's collection was returned to where it came from," the case agent told him.

"Chloe said Sylvie handled the transfers. She must have sold the collection instead, on the sly," Zach said. "Have you checked the Sheridan woman's bank accounts? If she had big deposits around the time the art was supposedly returned to South America, that would be conclusive evidence she's involved."

"Maybe. As long as the money stayed in her account and didn't get transferred to your girlfriend. They could be in this together."

"But why would Chloe need the letters? She was selling things that belonged to her."

"And to her mother. Didn't you say it was her mother who wanted to give the collection away?"

"Yes, but—"

"Well, maybe Miss Betancourt didn't agree with her mother. I'll grant you that Sylvie Sheridan is a possible perpetrator. We're still checking her out. I know she claimed to be from New York, but so far we haven't found any trace of her background there. All the records we've turned up so far start here in New Orleans, about fifteen years ago. Before that—zip."

"That's suspicious, don't you think? Where did she get the money to open her gallery?"

"Don't know. But the Betancourt woman isn't off the hook, not yet. Stick with your undercover role, at least until the shipment arrives on Friday. That should end the investigation, one way or another. Have you got your surveillance planned?"

"Yeah. I'll play a few games of checkers with the watchman. Then I'll act like I'm leaving, but I'll hide out in the warehouse instead."

"That should work. We'll have the surveillance van parked around the corner with your backup. Unless..."

Zach's ears perked up. "Unless what?"

"We've got a tip that there may be a shipment of cocaine coming in from Mexico by plane on Friday.

If that goes down, all available agents will be assigned to that investigation. The S.A.C. says drugs take priority over smuggled art."

"No kidding. When will you know about the drugs?"

"In a day or two. If we can't supply you with backup, I want you to treat this as a sneak-and-peek trip only. Watch and learn, but don't, I repeat, *do not* try to take the smugglers down all by yourself."

"So my assignment may not be over by Friday, after all."

"That's right. Don't let it get to you, Steele. At the very least, you'll know who picks up the goods from the warehouse."

"That may be enough. Look for a connection between the Sheridan woman and Cox, in the meantime. If she is the perp, chances are he's her customer."

"Will do. By the way, we haven't found any connection between Chloe and Cox before he invited her to his reception. Nor is there any evidence that Cox knew Charles Betancourt. Talk to you later."

Zach hung up the telephone. So he might be on his own Friday night. He could deal with that. But Chloe's cancellation of their dinner date nagged at him.

What did she have planned for Friday night?

Chloe left work late Friday afternoon, as soon as she'd learned that the new shipment from the *finca* had been delivered to the Betancourt warehouse.

Finally she would learn who had been tampering

with her shipments. Assuming they did it one more time. And provided she could stay awake that long. She hadn't gotten much sleep last night. The cocktail party Thursday evening had evolved into a late dinner, and then some of the crowd had decided to go dancing. She couldn't pass up the opportunity to nestle in Zachary's arms one more time. But they hadn't gotten home until after one o'clock, and she'd had trouble falling asleep.

Chloe knew Zachary wanted her. She couldn't have mistaken his physical reaction to her nearness while they'd danced. But when he'd brought her home, he'd refused her invitation to come up for coffee. What could be making him so reluctant to start an affair?

Shaking her head, Chloe pushed thoughts of Zachary to the back of her mind. She could only hope they would stay there. She'd been spending an awful lot of time thinking about him lately. But tonight she had other business to concentrate on.

After a light dinner and a longer nap than she'd planned, Chloe hurriedly got ready for her trip to the warehouse, muttering to herself as she dressed. "It's almost midnight—I should have been there before now. Why didn't I set the alarm?"

She tugged on black leggings, then added a black knit turtleneck. Shoving her feet into black ballet slippers, she slipped out her door and down the stairs. She didn't go through the lobby, choosing instead to exit the building by the service entrance at the rear.

She hadn't told anyone her plans for the evening—not even Joe Jester, the night watchman. It was possible, even probable, that nothing at all unusual was going to happen this time. But if it did, she had to assume Joe was most likely involved. Twice before, the shipment from Colombia had been disturbed. Twice before, there had been no signs of forced entry at the warehouse.

She didn't want to think that one of her employees was betraying her, but she couldn't ignore the facts. And Joe wasn't exactly her employee. Like most of the people who worked for Betancourt Coffees, he had been hired by her father, years ago. Until the recent episodes, Chloe had no reason to question the loyalty of any of the people who worked for her. But since someone had been interfering with the coffee shipments from Colombia, she had to suspect everyone, including Joe.

He'd been very upset when the torn bags had been discovered. Upset, and maybe a little remorseful. Because he'd let people into the warehouse after hours? At the very least, he must have been sleeping on the job.

She still didn't understand why anyone would rip open bags of coffee beans. At first she'd suspected someone might be contaminating the beans somehow. But why only a few bags? And why make it obvious that the bags had been opened? In any event, that had proven not to be the case. She'd had the coffee beans tested and no evidence of contamination had been found.

That left vandalism. Chloe equated vandals with teenagers, which was why she was not afraid to face them alone. The culprits hadn't hurt anyone or done any real damage. They'd only made a mess, and a minor mess at that. Chloe had planned to be on hand tonight to see for herself exactly who was responsible, and to call them to task for their shenanigans.

Chloe's footsteps faltered and slowed. Juvenile delinquents might not like being scolded. Maybe she should have brought a man along, after all.

But who? Not Zachary. While not as weak as she'd thought, he still had a limp. Plus, he'd had a long week, taking her here and there after business hours. She'd have to remember to credit him with overtime when she got to the office on Monday.

Chloe picked up her pace as she neared the warehouse. She planned to use the alley door, the one that opened between the storage rooms, for her entry. She'd never realized how dark that alley was at night. She plunged into the darkness, not giving herself time for any more second thoughts. She ran her fingers lightly along the stucco wall to guide her through the inky darkness.

The sound of her heart pounding grew louder as the blackness deepened, and she had to remind herself to breathe. "Fear is good," she muttered. "Keeps you alert." When she felt the door frame, Chloe pulled the key from her sweater pocket. She fumbled with it for a few seconds before she found the keyhole. Pushing the door open, she crept into the warehouse, her thin-soled slippers making no sound on the concrete floor.

Windows high in the warehouse walls allowed

enough moonlight to enter so that she could make out the stacks of coffee bags. Chloe couldn't tell if any of them had been moved. She was almost sure no one else was in the warehouse—not unless they were lurking in the deep shadows where the pale light from the new moon didn't penetrate.

Her heartbeat slowed, and her breathing became automatic again. So far, not bad. She reached the office, guided by the strip of light spilling from under the closed door. Were Joe and his cohorts inside, plotting more mysterious and nefarious acts? Chloe put her ear to the door and listened. Nothing. No sound at all, not even from the television.

Perhaps Joe was making his rounds. Chloe stepped away from the door and looked around one more time. Except for the office and the small bathroom that opened off of it, the warehouse was one large room with no place to hide, except among the bags of coffee beans stacked on pallets. If Joe were out there, she'd see his flashlight. Or he'd have turned the lights on.

Her hand hovered over the light switch next to the office. When she heard the moan, she hit the switch. Bright light flooded the warehouse. She could see at a glance that some of the bags had been ripped open. The floor around several of the pallets was covered with gray-green coffee beans.

"Shoot! I missed them."

Joe had some explaining to do. She shoved open the office door.

"Oh, my God!"

Joe was slumped over, his head resting on the checkerboard sitting on his desk. That she might have expected.

But not the other body, sprawled on the floor next to the desk. "Zachary?" She knelt beside him. "What's wrong with you?"

Putting her ear to his chest, she heard a steady heartbeat. Letting out her breath in a relieved whoosh, she jumped up and reached for the telephone. She dialed 9-1-1.

Hours later, Chloe sat next to a gurney in one of the cubicles of Ochsner Hospital's emergency room. She held Zachary's hand and murmured soothing words. Not that he heard her. He hadn't regained consciousness.

The doctor pulled aside the curtain. "We've got the lab results. Your employees were drugged. They both drank coffee laced with chloral hydrate—knockout drops."

"Will they be all right?"

"Yes. We're transferring Mr. Jester to the hospital for observation because of his age, but Mr. Steele is free to go as soon as he wakes up."

"I'm awake," Zachary rasped, opening his eyes a slit. "Wha' happened?"

"You drank drugged coffee, Zachary. How do you feel?"

"Groggy. And my throat hurts."

"That's because we put a tube down it to pump out your stomach," explained the doctor.

"Oh, Zachary, you must feel awful." Chloe patted his hand. "Maybe you should stay in the hospital tonight, too."

"No!" Zach struggled into a sitting position. "I hate hospitals."

The doctor grinned. "A lot of people feel that way. Let me check your vital signs one more time. If they're okay, you can leave now. Is there someone at home who can keep an eye on you?"

"Me. I can take care of myself." He flopped back down, closing his eyes.

"I don't think so, Zachary." Chloe smiled at his prone form. "I'll take him home with me, Doctor."

The doctor lifted the stethoscope from Zach's chest. "Good. He'll be groggy and confused for a few more hours—just watch him so he doesn't fall and hurt himself."

"Where are his clothes?" Chloe asked. She hadn't been allowed in the cubicle while the doctors were pumping Zach's stomach. Now he was wearing only an ill-fitting hospital gown.

An orderly found the bundle of clothes and helped Zach dress while Chloe called for a cab and located a wheelchair. A short taxi ride later, Chloe and the doorman took him to her apartment by way of the freight elevator.

"Thanks, Frank. I can take it from here," Chloe said as she opened her apartment door. She steered Zachary toward the bedroom. Propping him against the wall, she turned down her bed.

"Whatcha doin'?" Zach asked as he slid slowly down the wall.

Chloe dropped the quilt and grabbed for Zach, stopping him before he reached the floor. With her arms around his waist, she dragged him toward the bed. "Putting you to bed."

"Not sleepy." Zach yawned, then fell backward onto the bed.

"Zachary! You can't sleep in your clothes. For one thing, you won't be comfortable, and for another thing, they need washing."

A gentle snore was his only response.

"Oh, all right. I'll undress you." Chloe bit her bottom lip. Hard. The thought of taking Zachary's clothes off had sent a jolt of sexual awareness straight to her core.

What kind of woman was she?

The poor man was unconscious. She'd said she would take care of him, not take advantage of him. She couldn't do that, not when he was out cold.

Could she?

Should she?

With a brisk negative shake of her head, Chloe answered her own questions. Of course not. She'd get his clothes off, put them in the washer and then she'd…find something else to do until morning. Glancing out the window, she realized morning wasn't far off. Luckily for Zachary and her own self-esteem, she was too tired for hanky-panky with an unconscious man.

Chloe removed Zachary's running shoes and socks.

Then, taking a fortifying breath, sat on the edge of the bed and began working his navy blue sweater up his chest and over his head. Getting his arms free was the most difficult part, but she finally accomplished it.

Bare-chested, Zach did not look the least bit scrawny.

Chloe averted her eyes from his muscular torso. A woman could only resist so much temptation. She reached for his zipper. Sliding it down slowly, so as not to damage anything important, she felt her breathing grow short.

"Got it," she gasped as she finished unzipping his black jeans. She shoved the jeans down his hair-roughened legs and jerked them off. Clutching them to her breast, she gazed at Zachary.

Sprawled almost naked on her bed, he was the most beautiful man she'd ever seen. Broad shoulders, muscular chest, narrow waist... Her gaze slid downward. Zachary was perfect.

Except for the ugly red scar on his left thigh. Chloe winced when she saw it. "Oh, my, that must have hurt. No wonder you have a limp." Stroking his thigh, she felt the rough ridge of scar tissue. Funny, she'd thought he'd been injured in an automobile accident, but the scar was round, with jagged edges. What kind of wound left a mark like that?

Zachary groaned, and Chloe jerked her hand off his leg.

She got up quickly and pulled the covers up to his chin. Taking his clothes with her, she retreated to the kitchen. Once Zachary's clothes were in the washer, she sat down at the kitchen table.

She was trembling all over. "Delayed reaction," she murmured. From her adventure, not from having Zachary Steele right where she wanted him. She hadn't had time to think, much less react, since she'd found Joe and Zachary unconscious at the warehouse.

She needed to think about that. Who could have drugged the coffee? Why? Why had bags of coffee beans been ripped open for the third time? Figuring out answers to those questions would keep her busy for hours. Days.

But her busy little brain wasn't interested in speculating about coffee beans and criminals. It was spinning fantasies about the man she'd left in her bedroom.

In her bed.

Naked.

Unconscious.

She could do anything she wanted to with him.

Chloe hid her suddenly hot face in her hands. No, she couldn't. There were rules about this sort of thing. Rules made by men to protect women.

Rules that some men broke.

Not a man like Zachary, though. If the situation were reversed, if she were the one lying in his bed, he wouldn't dream of stripping her completely naked. A gentleman would never fantasize about a slow and delicious exploration of her body, first with his eyes, then with his hands. He wouldn't quiver in anticipation of tasting every square inch of her heated flesh while she lay there disoriented and helpless to resist.

No, Zachary wouldn't do any of those things.

Not unless she ordered him to. And she wouldn't do that. He was *not* her gigolo. She had to stop thinking of him that way. It was fast becoming an obsession.

Chloe got up from the kitchen table. She needed a shower, cold, and a few hours' rest before she could deal sensibly with coffee bean burglars and drugged employees and lust.

Especially lust.

After a quick shower, Chloe pulled her soft cotton nightshirt over her head and tiptoed to the bed. Zachary was still on his back, one hand flung over his head, the other curled on his chest. He was sound asleep, but she couldn't be sure if it was a natural sleep and not the aftereffects of a Mickey Finn. That meant he was still off limits. Untouchable.

With a sigh of regret, Chloe took a pillow from the bed, got a blanket from the armoire and headed for the living area. She arranged the blanket on one of the twin love seats that faced the fireplace and lay down.

Her feet dangled over the end of the love seat.

Twisting around, she curled up in a fetal position. Her knees hung over the edge of the cushions. Chloe rolled onto her back, keeping her knees bent. It was an excruciatingly uncomfortable position for someone who always slept on her stomach. She managed to stay in it for at least five minutes before turning over and stretching out her cramped legs.

Her feet dangled over the end of the love seat.

Chloe sat up and shoved her hair out of her face. "What am I going to do? I have to get some sleep." She looked around the room, but the other furniture—two bar stools and a rocking chair—looked even less like a bed than the love seat. "I need a bed. I have to have a bed!"

She picked up the pillow and walked purposefully toward her bedroom, guided by the city lights outside the windows. Whispering softly to herself, Chloe entered her bedroom. "I am not going to bother Zachary. I won't touch him. It's a big bed. Queen-size. He'll never even know I'm there."

Fluffing the pillow, she placed it carefully on the bed, lifted the covers and slid between them.

Zachary didn't stir. Just as she'd predicted, he didn't know she was there. She knew exactly where he was, however, and precisely how many centimeters separated them. Her breath came in shallow gasps, and every muscle in her body tensed in anticipation of...what?

Did she think Zachary would waken, find her next to him and be overcome with desire? She snorted. That sort of thing only happened in romance novels. Zachary would probably freak if he woke up now. If any of the drug lingered in his system, the shock of finding himself in bed with his boss might even be dangerous. He could fall out of bed.

Maybe that was an occupational hazard for a gigolo. Chloe fell asleep with a smile on her face.

7

Zach opened one eye and searched for the source of the loud ringing. It was a telephone on an unfamiliar nightstand next to the strange bed he was lying on. Still half-asleep, he reached for it. "Yeah?"

Silence.

"Hello?" Zach stared at the small hand resting on his abdomen. What the—

"Mr. Steele, is that you?"

"Yeah. Who's this?"

"Cox. Gerald Cox. We met last week."

"I remember. What can I do for you?"

Cox cleared his throat. "Is Miss Betancourt there?"

Zach turned his head. Damn. She was. There. In bed with him. How had that happened? "She is."

"May I speak with her?"

"She's asleep. We had kind of a late night. Can I take a message?"

"Of course. I wanted to ask her—the two of you, to join me for breakfast at Brennan's this morning. We can discuss rescheduling my tour of her company. Will that be convenient?"

"I don't know. I'll get back to you as soon as she wakes up."

Zach hung up the telephone. Chloe was on her stomach, her face turned toward him, but shielded by a silky mass of tangled blond hair. He pushed it away from her eyes. They were shut tight. "Chloe. Wake up."

He poked her shoulder. She turned onto her side and pulled the pillow on top of her head. "Uh-uh."

Zach took the pillow away from her and poked her again. Harder. "Ms. Betancourt. Wake up! You've got some explaining to do."

She raised her head and opened her eyes a slit. "Go away." The words were delivered in something of a snarl. Mumbling vulgarities about morning people, Chloe closed her eyes again, and pulled the covers over her head.

He jerked the quilt off of her. "Wake up, Chloe. We have to talk. Why am I in your bed?"

Slitting her eyes open, she rolled onto her back. "Nothing happened. I didn't lay a hand on you. Give me back my quilt. I'm cold."

"No. Tell me, Chloe. What am I doing here?"

She wiggled into a sitting position and gazed at him. "Don't you remember?"

"No."

"You don't remember being at the hospital? Having your stomach pumped? Someone slipped you a Mickey Finn last night."

"Someone? Or you?"

"Me? Why would I—oh, no. You can't suspect me of drugging you to get you into my bed?"

Zach leaned against the headboard and closed his eyes. Pieces of memories from the previous night were surfacing. None of them made him proud of himself. He'd blown it. He groaned.

"Zachary, are you all right?"

He felt her soft hands on his shoulders, on his forehead. He groaned again. "No. I feel sick."

"I'll call the doctor. I knew you should have stayed at the hospital."

"I don't want to go to the hospital. I hate hospitals."

"That's what you said last night. That's why I brought you home with me. You were too groggy to be by yourself."

"Yeah, right. You wanted me here."

"I did. So I could take care of you."

"That's why you were in bed with me? So you could watch me sleep?"

"Yes. No. This is the only bed I've got. I tried sleeping on the love seat, but it's too short. Even for me."

"Oh. You couldn't sleep on the floor?"

"No, I couldn't. If you're through acting like a Victorian maiden who's been compromised, can we get on with our discussion?"

"Maiden?" Insulted, Zach crossed his arms across his chest. It was that or grab her and show her just how "maidenly" he was feeling. "We are compromised. Both of us. Gerald Cox called this morning and I answered the telephone. He knows we're sleeping together."

"We are not sleeping together! We slept together."

"That's what I said."

"You implied that something went on. Nothing happened, Zachary." She narrowed her eyes. "What difference would it make anyway? He thinks we're engaged?"

"Where are my clothes? I don't remember taking them off."

"I undressed you. I washed your clothes. I'll get them for you." She leaped off the bed, and raced from the room.

Taking a few deep breaths, Zach leaned against the headboard and looked around the room. High ceilings, crisscrossed with pipes and beams, brick walls and large windows on one wall belied its past as a warehouse. Somehow, the colorful prints on the walls, the homey quilt on the bed, made it a cozy, comfortable room. A room a man could get used to spending time in.

With Chloe.

Chloe, the suspect. Chloe, the woman who'd been at the warehouse last night, the same night the smugglers recovered their loot from the bags of coffee beans. The Chloe who had every opportunity to slip a few drops of chloral hydrate into the night watchman's coffeepot. That Chloe.

She returned with a steaming mug of coffee. "Here. I remembered to set the timer on the coffeepot last night, but I forgot to put your clothes in the dryer. It won't take them long to dry, though."

"Where's your coffee?"

"In the kitchen."

"I don't think I want any." He'd kill for one sip.

"For heaven's sake. You think this coffee is drugged, too?" She took a big swallow. "Here. I don't know why you're so suspicious."

He took the mug from her. Taking a fortifying sip of coffee, Zach said, "Thanks, I needed that."

"Do you remember what happened?" Chloe asked, sitting on the edge of the bed, facing him.

"I remember going to the warehouse—"

"Why? I never thought to ask."

Zach thought fast. Not any easy task when his brain felt as cottony as his mouth. "Insomnia. One of the side effects of my accident. I've spent a few nights at the warehouse playing checkers with Joe."

"I saw the checkerboard. I didn't know you liked board games."

Zach shrugged negligently. "It was a way to pass the time. I didn't have anything better to do—you canceled our dinner date, remember?"

"I remember. And you and Joe had a cup of coffee while you played checkers?"

"Yeah. I think so. I'm a little hazy on what happened after I got to the warehouse." Zach rubbed his forehead. Chloe's questions were giving him a headache. It was time to change the direction of the interrogation. "Why were you there?"

She turned pink. "Promise you won't laugh at me."

He nodded, trying to work up a little professional skepticism. Not easy to do, when Chloe was so close. And so underdressed. She probably thought her nightshirt covered her decently, but the soft cotton molded to every curve on her sexy little body. "Shouldn't you get dressed?"

"I will. In a minute. Move over." She swung her feet onto the bed, then leaned against the headboard, next to him. "About last night. I was playing detective. And not very well. I overslept, so I got there too late, after the damage was done."

"Damage?" Zach tried to concentrate. Having Chloe beside him on the bed was making his brain fog up again. "What damage?"

"Someone's been tampering with the coffee shipments from Colombia. I thought it was kids, because they never took anything. They just ripped open a few bags of coffee beans. It's happened twice before, and I wanted to catch them in the act."

Zach's brain cleared in an instant. He was outraged. "You were going to face criminals alone?"

"Joe was there, and teenagers—"

"Teenagers these days have been known to pack automatic weapons. To kill people."

"Oh, no, surely not. Not over a few bags of coffee."

Grabbing her by the shoulders, he gave her a good shake. "Listen to me, Chloe Betancourt! Don't you ever do anything that foolish again. Do you understand me?"

"Y-yes. What's got into you, Zachary?" She stared at him, wide-eyed. "You're so...forceful."

Carefully, he loosened his grip on her shoulders, finger by finger. "Sorry. It must be an aftereffect of being drugged." He had to get back in character, but it wasn't easy. He sure as hell didn't feel like a mild-mannered male secretary.

Chloe had just taken another big step away from being the primary target of his investigation. He'd wanted to protect her when she'd been number one on the list of suspects. Now he wanted to lock her up, but not in jail. In a bedroom. Alone. With him. "Did you see anyone when you got to the warehouse?"

"No. Only you and Joe. Unconscious." She leaned her forehead against his shoulder. "Oh, Zachary, for a moment, I thought you were d-dead."

Zach gave up and let his arms do what they wanted to do, which was to wrap tightly around Chloe. He pulled her close. "There, there, honey, babe. I'm all right."

"Wh-what if it was smugglers? They might have k-killed you."

"Smugglers?" Zach stiffened.

Chloe raised her head, her eyes troubled. "I thought maybe—Colombia doesn't only export coffee, you know. Drugs could be involved. The police think so. Detective Brown said they'd have the canine unit check out the warehouse, but I haven't heard from him yet." She reached for the telephone. "I'm going to call him right now."

Zach grabbed her hand. "Detective? You called the police? When?"

"As soon as I found you and Joe."

"Why did you call the police?"

"Someone had hurt you. The warehouse had been broken into for the third time—"

"You didn't call the police the first two times."

"No." Tilting her head, she eyed him curiously. "How did you know that?"

"I didn't know." Zach cursed to himself. He knew because it had been noted in Chloe's dossier. "I assumed. Since no one had checked for drugs before. Either in the bags of coffee or in Joe's coffeepot."

"Oh. Well, you're right. We didn't call them before because nothing was taken. Joe never mentioned falling asleep on the job. And I misspoke when I said the place had been broken into. There never has been any breaking and entering. Whoever is doing this has a key. Remind me to have the locks changed, Zachary. I should have thought of that before, but I didn't expect it to happen again and again. I don't understand what's going on, but I'm getting to the bottom of it, if I—"

"No, you're not." He jerked her back into his arms. "Not a chance. I will not have you putting yourself in danger!"

"Oh, Zachary. It's very sweet of you to be concerned."

"Sweet again, huh?"

"As sugar, Sugar." She managed a shaky grin as she got off the bed. "I'll get your clothes."

Chloe dressed while Zachary showered. Having a man in her shower was almost as interesting as having one in her bed. Zachary had layers. He seemed diffident and willing to follow her lead most of the time. But there were times when he definitely took charge.

Or tried to. She grinned. He was kind of cute when he got all forceful and bossy. Telling her to fix breakfast, for instance. As if he thought that was a woman's job. As soon as she'd reminded him who worked for whom, he'd gotten all flustered and apologetic. He'd actually blushed when he'd said he was sorry.

Definitely cute.

Sweet, too, the way he'd gotten so protective when she'd said she was going to get to the bottom of the coffee bean caper. Zachary was turning out to be her ideal man in the flesh—nice, cute, sweet. And unpredictable enough not to be boring. She hadn't meant to include "dull" as one of her dream man's characteristics, but in retrospect, a man incapable of surprising a woman now and then would be exactly that.

Too bad he'd woken up before her. She would have enjoyed spending a few minutes watching him sleep. She hadn't realized how different a night's growth of beard made a man look. Zachary had gone from clean-cut boy-next-door to scruffy, sexy man in a matter of hours. Fascinating.

Too bad he'd been so groggy last night. She might have completed his seduction if he'd been awake enough to know what was going on. Still, it had to be only a matter of time before she reached her goal. Zachary had gotten downright protective when she'd talked about solving the mystery of the mutilated coffee bean bags. That had to be a good sign.

"Chloe? Where are my clothes?"

"Right here." Chloe handed the jeans to Zachary around the partially opened bathroom door, and she dropped his sweater onto the bed. Steam from the shower would only get it damp again, she virtuously assured herself. Grinning at her reflection in the mirror, she acknowledged that seeing Zach's muscular shoulders and chest bare one more time would be a definite bonus.

A few minutes later, while she was carefully stroking her naturally pale lashes with mascara, he strolled into her bedroom. Hair damp, naked to the waist, he looked anything but sweet—sexy was the word that came to mind. Chloe almost poked her eye out with the mascara wand. "Ouch."

"What's wrong?"

"Nothing." She finished applying the mascara while Zachary sat on her bed, putting on his socks and running shoes.

Chloe found the scene almost unbearably intimate. They could be an old married couple.

Married? Where had that thought come from? She wanted an affair, not a lifelong commitment.

Clearing her suddenly dry throat, she said, "Breakfast is ready. I found some banana-nut muffins in the freezer. And I made a fresh pot of coffee."

Zachary pulled his sweater over his head. "Lead the way, boss lady."

Chloe breathed for the first time since he'd entered the bedroom partially unclothed. Maybe she should stop playing games with him. Serious matters were afoot, and this might not be the right time for fooling around with the hired help.

On the other hand, she might never have another employee so willing to please.

She waited until Zachary had finished his third muffin before bringing up their warehouse adventure.

"I called Detective Brown while you were in the shower. He said there were no traces of drugs in the warehouse. He said my guess was probably the right answer—teenagers. In his opinion, the most they could be charged with is criminal trespass. I got the definite impression solving this crime isn't going to be a top priority with the New Orleans Police Department."

"Maybe not. Trespass isn't a serious crime compared with murder and armed robbery."

"But you were drugged! That should make it serious. Isn't that attempted murder or something?"

"Probably not. Nobody came close to dying. And Joe must have been drugged during the two previous incidents. He recovered both times—without having his stomach pumped."

"Yes. So that means whoever's doing this knows exactly what dosage will knock someone out for a few hours, with no side effects. Who has that kind of knowledge?"

"Anyone with access to the Internet would be my guess. This is the information age."

She sipped her coffee. "I hadn't thought about that. But how did they get the chloral hydrate into the coffeepot?"

"I can think of only one way—someone put the drug in the water reservoir. The dosage would have been diluted when Joe filled the coffeemaker with water."

"Seems kind of hit-and-miss to me. How could they know how many cups Joe planned to make?"

"They probably based the amount of the chloral hydrate on a full pot. If Joe made less than that, he'd just get a bigger dose and a longer nap."

Chloe shuddered. "Maybe a forever kind of nap. This sounds less and less like vandals to me. It's too...calculated. But if it's not teenagers, who could it be?"

Zachary shrugged. "Beats me."

"Emile Arcenaux, I suppose. Playing dirty tricks on me is one of his favorite pastimes." She stood. "Don't get up, Zachary. Have another muffin and finish your coffee. I have to call the hospital and check on Joe. I owe him an apology. I actually suspected him of being involved somehow. I should have known that no one who works for me would be that underhanded and sneaky."

Zach's face grew warm, an increasingly common occurrence around Chloe. And he felt a twinge of something that might have been guilt, except that "underhanded and sneaky" was what his real employer paid him to be.

Chloe walked to the telephone on the kitchen wall. "And I have to call a security company and arrange for someone to take Joe's place until he's recovered. I need to return Mr. Cox's call, too."

Setting his empty cup on the table, Zach stood. "I think I'll take a walk to the warehouse and have a look around. Maybe the police missed something."

"That's a good idea. Wait until I make those calls and I'll go with you."

Zach poured himself another cup of coffee and sat down again. While Chloe called the hospital and a rent-a-cop place, he tried reviewing Friday night's activities objectively, starting with his own sorry performance. The case agent was not going to be pleased that his ace U.C.A. ended up in the emergency room having his stomach pumped.

That didn't bother him as much as his own sloppiness. He couldn't blame his carelessness on his marginal physical condition. There never had been anything wrong with his head—before he met Chloe Betancourt. She turned his brain to mush. He should have spent his time tailing Chloe last night, instead of drinking drugged coffee. Then he would know for sure if she'd arrived at the warehouse before or after the damage had been done.

From now on, he'd stick to her closer than mold on week-old bread. He'd check everything about this case six ways from Sunday. Starting with the torn bags. How did the smugglers know which bags to rip open?

Chloe hung up the telephone. "That's taken care of."

"Are you ready to go?"

She looked at the clock on the wall. "In a few minutes. My mother calls me every Saturday around this time. She'll want a report on the wedding preparations."

The telephone rang. Chloe grinned at him. "See? Why don't you have another cup of coffee, and read the paper." She picked up the receiver. "Hi, Mom! How are you?"

Zach left his coffee cup on the table. He'd had enough caffeine for one morning. He picked up the paper, but none of the headlines grabbed his attention. He couldn't stop thinking about Chloe. As much as he wanted to, he couldn't give her the benefit of the doubt, not yet. He was almost sure Chloe was innocent, but her explanation of why she'd appeared at the warehouse didn't hold up to close scrutiny. A little thing like her, five feet nothing, prepared to face down miscreants all alone? Not likely.

And Chloe would have had the best opportunity to slip a few drops of chloral hydrate into the coffeemaker. She wouldn't have needed to break and enter her own warehouse. She had a key.

In her favor, she had called the police this time. Her concern about him and Joe had seemed genuine. As had her indignation when she'd thought someone was using her coffee to smuggle cocaine into the country.

He'd managed to scan the sports page by the time Chloe returned to the living room. She was beaming.

"You look happy."

"It must be contagious. Mother is giddy with happiness. I'm ashamed I even thought about telling her I did not approve of her marrying again. Like arranging her life is my job." Shaking her head, Chloe walked to the closet by the front door and took out a jacket. "Are you ready?"

"Yeah. But you don't have to go."

"It's my warehouse. And looking for clues isn't in your job description. Why are you so interested?"

Zach took the jacket and held it for her. "When someone slips me a Mickey Finn, I just naturally get a little curious."

The warehouse was silent when they entered through the alley door. While Chloe got a broom and swept up the spilled beans, Zach gathered up the torn bags. There were eleven in all. Each had a Velásquez logo stenciled on the burlap, but so did the bags that hadn't been opened. How did the smugglers know which bags to search?

"What's that?"

"What?"

"That red string." He stooped and picked up a piece. "Where did that come from?"

"It was on the floor with the coffee beans, under one of the pallets."

Zach checked the other bags. None were closed with red string. Whoever placed the stolen artwork in the bags closed them with red string, not brown. That was how the receivers of the stolen goods knew which bags contained the stolen artifacts. He looked around again, and checked the loose beans Chloe had swept into a pile. Eleven bags had been opened, but only one strand of red string had been left behind. Whoever the smugglers were, they were careful.

"What's in the storerooms? More coffee?"

"No. Sylvie uses one to store some artwork she doesn't have room for at the gallery."

"Artwork? Shouldn't that sort of thing be stored somewhere less..."

"Grubby?"

"I was thinking of the summer—the heat and humidity."

"Trust me. The things Sylvie stores here couldn't be hurt by heat or cold. Want to see?"

"Sure."

Chloe went to the office and recovered a key from the desk drawer. She unlocked the padlock and opened the door to the storeroom. Flicking a light switch, she stood aside and let Zach see the contents of the room.

Two large bare breasts came into view. "Good Lord. I didn't know your friend dealt in pornography."

"Please. That is art, not porn. It's a bronze sculpture in honor of an old Mardi Gras tradition."

"Of course. Show me your—"

"That's the one. A cry that will be heard with increasing frequency as the big day grows near. The first Mardi Gras parade is only a couple of weeks after Christmas."

"Does your friend think someone will buy that monstrosity?"

"Someday. She has photographs of it at the gallery, and of the other sculptures she stores here. Occasionally she brings someone here to see the real thing."

Zach stared at her. "So she has a key to the warehouse?"

"Yes."

"What's in the other storeroom? More artwork?"

"No. Only supplies, plastic barrels, things like that. I need one of the barrels to put the spilled beans in." Chloe opened the second storeroom.

Zach took out the barrel she pointed to. "Can you still use the beans?"

"Oh, yes. They have to be washed before they're roasted anyway. That's what makes this whole thing so confusing. Nothing is taken, nothing is destroyed. If it weren't for you and Joe being drugged, there wouldn't be any harm done at all."

"It's a mystery, all right."

A knock sounded on the street door. Zach opened it, and found a uniformed guard standing on the sidewalk.

Chloe put the lid on the barrel she'd filled with coffee beans, gave the guard a few instructions, and declared herself ready to go.

"I'll walk you home."

"That's not necessary. Are you sure you're recovered? Maybe you should take a taxi home."

"I'm okay. And I have to go right by your place to get to mine. What are you going to do for the rest of the day?"

"Go over the presentation I plan to give Mr. Cox while we're cruising up the Mississippi next week. That way he'll know what we can offer even before he tours the company."

"Can I help?"

"It's Saturday. I couldn't ask you to work any more overtime. Besides, you need to take it easy for a day or two. I want you completely well when we're on that yacht. Speaking of which, don't you have to pack for the trip?"

"Packing for a two-day cruise won't take that long. I don't mind hanging around if you want me to. What's a personal assistant for?"

"Marie would never put up with this. Her family's too important to her. As it should be."

"You think families should take precedence over business?"

"I guess so. Provided you have a family."

"You have your mother, and you'll have a stepfather in a couple of weeks."

"Yes, but...that's not the same as a husband and children."

"Do you want a husband and children?"

"No. Definitely not. Do you? Want to get married someday?"

"I suppose I do. My parents certainly expect it. They're big on family."

"That must make the estrangement from your sister especially hard for them."

"Estrangement?"

"Oh, sorry. That's none of my business."

"Why would you think we're estranged?"

"You get a funny look on your face when you talk about her. Which isn't often. And you said she doesn't come home for holidays."

"That's geography. Nothing else."

"Oh. Well, if you don't mind, I could use an audience."

Chloe made her presentation, pointing out the advantages of a specialty coffee supplier, one small enough to be able to roast to order so that the product was fresh each day, yet large enough to have the capacity to fill orders promptly.

"You should have his signature on a contract by the time we get back to New Orleans."

"I hope so. Getting the contract with Cox's Coffee Emporiums would sure make things easier."

"You wouldn't have to work so hard."

"I don't find the work hard, exactly. Just time-consuming. There never seems to be enough hours to do everything I need to do, much less things I only want to do."

"Too bad the cruise up the river is business. You sound like a woman in need of a vacation."

Or an affair.

8

Monday morning, Chloe let Zachary assist her from the taxi they'd taken from her apartment to the dock where Gerald Cox's yacht was anchored. She stared at the elegant vessel. "My goodness. The *Caffeine Queen* is more than a yacht. It's almost as big as a cruise ship."

"Not quite," said Zach. "But she's in the super-yacht class, all right."

"Are you sure you're going to be all right? Do you have Dramamine?"

"There are no waves on the river. I'll be okay. Trust me."

"Welcome aboard." Gerald Cox was standing at the head of the gangplank, waiting to usher them aboard. A uniformed crew member stood next to him. "The Arcenauxs arrived a few minutes ago. Marian is taking them on a tour. Shall we join them?"

At Chloe's murmured assent, Cox ushered them into a spacious room. "This is the main salon. The dining room is forward, with the galley in between. My study is aft. You will notice we have plenty of room for sunbathing and lounging on this deck."

Chloe made appropriate admiring sounds. Zachary seemed very interested in Cox's explanations of the various amenities, she noticed.

"Thomas will see you to your cabin on the lower deck. We've put you two together—the *Queen* sleeps six, plus the crew, but only as long as three of the six sleep with the other three. I wasn't sure about you two, until I called your apartment and Mr. Steele answered the telephone. You don't mind bunking together, do you?"

"Not at all," murmured Chloe. Her cheeks felt a little warm, but she attributed that to excitement, not embarrassment. She would have Zachary alone in a tiny cabin for two whole nights.

Zachary handed their luggage to the steward. "Are all the cabins on the lower deck?"

"Yes, midships and astern. The crew quarters are forward."

The Arcenauxs appeared on deck, along with an attractive middle-aged woman. "You know Emile and Bette, Chloe. And this is my wife—Marian, meet Chloe Betancourt and her fiancé, Zachary Steele."

"How do you do?" Marian Cox waved her hand, shooing Zachary and Chloe after Thomas. "Let them get settled, Gerald. We're about to leave."

"Cocktails at five in the salon," said Cox, ushering them to the stairs. "Don't bother dressing for dinner. We keep things casual aboard the *Caffeine Queen*."

The Coxes' invitation had specified casual attire, but Chloe had chosen to wear a dress, a short, sexy swirl of red silk. It was not the kind of dress that called for conservative leather pumps. Chloe perched precariously on top of red stiletto heels. As for what she'd chosen to wear underneath...well, Zachary was in for a treat.

Zachary had obviously taken the invitation to mean business casual. He was wearing khaki slacks, a white shirt and tie, and a tweed sport coat.

Chloe and Zach followed Thomas to a cabin on the port side of the boat. Thomas opened the door, and placed their luggage inside.

Chloe looked around the cabin. "Not roomy, but larger than I expected. And very luxurious. Look at all that teak paneling—and the view. I thought boats had portholes, but that's a picture window." She stepped to the window and looked out. "I can see Algiers Point."

"We can't stay here." Zachary was staring at the double bed. "I assumed there would be bunk beds."

Chloe gave him a saucy grin. "We've slept together before. We can do it again."

"I think I'd better leave. I'm beginning to feel a little queasy, after all." He started backing out the door.

She grabbed his hand. "Zachary. We're still at the dock. Anyway, you were right. There aren't any waves on the river."

"I'm not staying here with you, Chloe. It's not right."

"Too late. We're moving." Chloe pulled Zachary farther into the room, nudging the door shut with her hip. She began unpacking their luggage.

Zachary sat in the cabin's lone chair, sulking.

"Get over it, Zachary. You'll spoil everything if you keep acting like this."

"Like what?"

"Like...I don't know what. Like someone who wants to be somewhere else."

"I'm not acting. I do want to be somewhere else."

"You started this. You got us engaged."

"The engagement is not real, Chloe."

"I know that. But Mr. Cox doesn't. You don't want me to lose out to Emile Arcenaux, do you? Isn't that why you agreed to come on the cruise with me?"

"Yes. But I didn't know we'd have to share a cabin. And a bed." Zachary scowled at the bed.

Chloe smiled. "You know the old saying, Zachary."

He turned the scowl on her. "You mean, I've made my bed and now I'll have to lie in it?"

"That's the one. What's wrong? I thought we had progressed beyond the employer-employee stage. I thought we had become...friends."

"We have. We are...friends. But that's as far as we should go. Until..."

"Until?"

"We get back to New Orleans." He turned his gaze away from her and muttered, "A few more days, that's all it should take to finish."

"Finish what? I don't know what you're talking about."

"Never mind," Zachary said, scowling at the view. The yacht was moving beneath the Crescent City

Connection, the twin span connecting the east and west banks of the river. "I don't like boats. Even without waves."

A ship's bell rang. "It's five o'clock. Time to join the Coxes and the Arcenauxs," said Chloe, taking Zachary by the arm. "Thank goodness the boat isn't big enough for Emile's cousins."

Burgeoning anticipation made each moment spent on drinking, dining and small talk feel like an hour. By the end of the evening, Chloe felt as though she'd been treading water all night. She was ready to *swim*.

"Good night, people. Breakfast at eight, but there will be coffee in the salon at six for any early birds." Gerald Cox beamed at his guests.

"And brunch for those who want to sleep in," added his wife. "We won't arrive at Oak Alley until around noon tomorrow."

"Lovebirds sleep in, don't we, dear?" Emile Arcenaux said, leering at his wife.

Chloe yawned delicately, hiding her impatience one more time. "I'm ready for bed," she murmured.

"I think I'll take a turn on deck," said Zachary, tugging at his shirt collar.

Chloe smothered a grin. Zachary was nervous, and she knew why. He had guessed what she planned to do to him as soon as they were alone.

"Not now, old man," said Cox, slapping Zachary on the back. "You'll get in the way. The crew is tying up for the night. Even if we wanted to keep moving, there's too much fog on the river to continue."

"Come along, Zachary," Chloe said, taking him

by the arm. Her hand trembled slightly. He wasn't the only one feeling a trifle anxious. She had good reason—she'd never seduced a man before. Any new challenge was bound to make a woman a little nervous.

Outside their cabin door, Zachary pulled free. "I'll wait here for a few minutes. Give you time to get ready for bed."

"Don't be silly. It's not like we haven't shared a bedroom before. We can get ready for bed together."

"The last time we did this I was unconscious, remember?" He followed her into the cabin, closing the door behind them.

The steward had turned down the bed and pulled the drapes over the window. The cabin lights had been dimmed to a romantic glow.

"Isn't this cozy?" sighed Chloe.

"Yeah. Cozy." Zachary leaned against the door. His dark eyes were unreadable.

He had to know what came next. She'd been seducing him for days now. Touching him, petting him, stealing kisses whenever the opportunity arose. He hadn't run screaming from her. Yet.

Her heart pounding, Chloe stepped in front of him. Sliding her hands around his neck, she stood on tiptoe and began kissing his square jaw, his chiseled cheekbones, his slightly bent nose.

Zach's hands went to her waist. For an anxious moment Chloe thought he would push her away. "Chloe," he groaned huskily. "Do you know what you're doing to me?"

"Anything I want?" she whispered, her mouth almost touching his.

His lips curved into a rueful grin. "Possibly."

She kissed him on the mouth, nibbling at his lips until they parted. Chloe explored the warm depths she'd gained access to with her tongue, thrusting and teasing until she got what she wanted.

Zachary tightened his hold on her, his hands dropping from her waist to her hips. "Probably. Be gentle with me, Chloe."

A sudden pang of conscience made her pause. "I need to tell you something."

"What?"

"My intentions are not honorable."

His eyes narrowed. "What does that mean?"

"This isn't about love. Or forever. Only pleasure. Only now."

He frowned at her. For an anxious moment, she thought he might not like her terms. Then, with a curt nod, he said, "I can live with that."

She let out the breath she hadn't realized she'd been holding. "Good. As long as we both understand that this is only temporary." Chloe kissed him on the chin and turned her back. "Unzip me, please." Her voice shook, but only a little.

Nothing happened. Zachary's hands rested lightly on her hips.

Glancing over her shoulder, she asked, "Well? You do know how to unzip, don't you? You just take that little tab at the top and pull."

Zachary unzipped the dress. Quickly. "There." He

tried walking around her, but Chloe turned and blocked his path. The dress slipped, baring her shoulders.

"Now, I'll help you undress." Her voice shook a little more. She slipped her hands under his lapels and slowly pushed the jacket off his shoulders. It fell to the floor. "I don't know why I ever thought of you as scrawny." She squeezed his biceps. "Feel those muscles. You have been working out." She untied his tie and began unbuttoning his shirt.

"Wait. Don't. Stop." Zachary sounded winded, as if he'd been running a long distance. "Chloe—"

Chloe put her fingers on his lips. "Hush. I'm not going to hurt you. I promise." Sliding her fingers to the nape of his neck, she pulled his head down until she could reach his mouth with hers. She kissed one corner of his mouth, then used her tongue to gently trace her way to the other corner. That was so much fun that she did it again, working her way back to the first spot she'd kissed.

He took a deep, shuddering breath. "I don't want to hurt you, either."

"I know that." Chloe continued unbuttoning his shirt.

He grabbed her hands. "I can do this. I don't need any help. I'm a big boy."

She pressed her lower body against his and wiggled. "Mmm. So you are. And getting bigger all the time."

"Chloe." Zach groaned. "You're going too far."

"Good. Too far is exactly where I want to go."

She slipped her hands from under his and pulled his shirttail out of the waistband of his trousers. Once the shirt had followed his jacket to the floor, Chloe took only a few seconds to admire Zachary's muscular chest. She had to hurry. He was obviously aroused, but she had the feeling he might talk himself out of it if she gave him time to think.

"Sit down and I'll take off your shoes." She gave him a gentle push, and Zach sat on the end of the bed.

Kneeling in front of him, Chloe removed one shoe, then the other. She slipped off his socks. "You have nice feet."

"Large."

"Well shaped." Still on her knees, Chloe unbuckled his belt, then reached for the zipper.

Zach grabbed her by the shoulders and pulled her to a standing position. "Stop that."

Pouting, she looked at him. "Don't you want me, Zachary?"

"No. Yes. But not yet. There are...things we need to discuss."

She shrugged the dress off her shoulders and let it slide to the floor at his bare feet. She wore a bra and panties made of lace and promises. A sexy garter belt, promising even more, held up her silk stockings.

Zach's knees appeared to buckle and he sat down again. Sitting next to him, she slowly unhooked the garters and slid the silky hose from one leg, then the other. "What was it you wanted to talk about?"

"What?"

Chloe could tell he was trying to keep his gaze straight ahead, but he was failing. He was staring at her legs. "You said there were things we needed to discuss."

"Yeah." He slowly raised his head. Chloe could feel his gaze leaving a burning trail from her ankles to her chin.

Chloe reached behind her and unhooked the garter belt. "What things?"

"Uh. I forget. I can't think when I look at—when you look at me like that." He stood so quickly that he almost jostled her off the bed. "Where is your nightgown? I'll get it for you. Then we'll talk."

"I didn't bring one."

"You didn't bring one?" Zachary's voice rose.

"I didn't bring one," she repeated, kicking off her stiletto heels and shimmying out of her hose.

"That's crazy, Chloe. It's December."

"I know what month it is, but the temperature was in the sixties today. Besides, I planned for you to keep me warm."

Zachary fumbled with the cabin door. He seemed to be having trouble finding the doorknob. "I'll see if Mrs. Cox has a spare."

"Zachary! Stop. You can't do that."

"You're right. It's late. They're probably in bed." He left the door, and without looking at her, sidled sideways until he reached the built-in dresser. He opened the dresser and took out a pair of pajamas.

Tossing the top over his shoulder in the general

direction of the bed, he said, "Here, you can sleep in this."

Chloe patted the mattress. "Later, maybe. Come here, Zachary. I want to finish undressing you."

Zach swallowed a groan. He wanted that, too. And he wanted the pleasure of relieving Chloe of her few remaining items of clothing. But... He was an agent. She was a target. He was sworn to uphold the law. This should not be happening.

Chloe *had* been a target, insisted a little voice in the back of his head. She was innocent. There was no law against making love to a beautiful, willing woman.

Yeah, but she might not be so eager to bed him if she knew he was an agent. He couldn't tell her that, not yet. She might feel a little annoyed once she found out he'd been deceiving her. *Annoyed?* Who was he kidding? She would be mad as hell.

"Zachary? Aren't you coming to bed?" For the first time in days, his little tyrant sounded unsure of her power over him. She had to know how he felt about her. Ever since the explosive kiss they'd shared at her house, he'd been following her around like a lovesick puppy.

Love? Nah. Never happen. Not to him.

Even as he tried to talk himself out of it, he knew it was true. He'd gone and done what countless secretaries before him had done.

He had fallen in love with his boss.

"Zachary. I demand that you come to bed this instant."

Reeling from the shock of discovering he was in love, Zach gave up his token resistance. It would take a stronger man than he to refuse such an imperious demand. How could he pass up being seduced by the woman he loved? Decision made, Zach turned toward the bed. Chloe opened her arms, beckoning him to her with a gesture as old as time.

Watching her closely, he unzipped his pants and shoved them off. Chloe's eyes widened, and her breathing sounded a little ragged. Good. He shouldn't be the only one having trouble getting enough oxygen.

Dressed only in his knit boxers, he joined her on the bed. He lay on his back, his arms crossed over his chest. He would surrender, but not right away. He might be a pushover, but he didn't want her to know that. A man had his pride. "All right. I'm in bed. Now what?"

"Don't you know?" She sounded startled.

"Why don't you show me?"

Chloe sat up and knelt beside him. Her gaze slid over him, from head to toe. Zach had to work hard to keep still. He wanted to grab her and show her he did know what came next, and what came after that and—

He sucked in his breath.

She'd stopped looking and started touching. Slowly, Chloe ran her hands over his chest, her fingers tangling in the hair on his chest. Her nails grazed his nipples and he twitched reflexively.

Chloe's hands stilled. "Did that hurt?"

"Ah, no," he said. "Not at all. You might want to do more of that."

"All right." She began moving her hands again, stroking his shoulders, rubbing his chest, caressing his abdomen. "Your stomach is as hard as a rock."

Chloe paused when her hands reached the scar on his thigh. "This is an odd scar. I noticed when I undressed you the last time. What—"

Zach reached for her hand. "Talk about hard. My stomach isn't the only place that's like a rock." He nudged her hand toward the bulge in his briefs.

Chloe's fingers found the spot. Grasping him gently, she said, "I think we have a problem."

"No, we don't," he said through clenched teeth. "What problem?"

"You're still dressed."

"Oh. That problem. You can take care of that."

She released him and slid his briefs down his legs and off. She took her time about it, driving Zach to the limits of his control.

"You're...still...dressed, too," he noted, gasping for breath.

"So I am. Want to fix that?"

"Oh, yeah." With greedy hands, he arranged her so that she lay sprawled on his chest. Reaching behind her back, he unhooked her bra. She raised up slightly, so that he could remove the garment. Her bare breasts spilled onto his chest. He could feel her nipples harden into tiny buds. "You'd better not regret this," he muttered just before his teeth closed on her earlobe.

"Never." She slid her arms over his chest. "Oh, Zachary. I've dreamed about this."

"So have I, sweetheart, so have I. Let's make a few dreams come true tonight."

Chloe took him at his word, slowly exploring his body with her hands and mouth, lingering at each new place she discovered until Zach thought he might die of pleasure. She was showing him erogenous zones he'd never known he had. She kissed him again and again, until he was writhing beneath her assault.

Zach fought his instinct to reverse their positions and take control of their lovemaking. He didn't need to be in control, not when following Chloe's lead in the sensuous dance that was giving him more pleasure than he'd ever known.

He tried his best to give pleasure for pleasure. He ran his hands lovingly down Chloe's slim back, reveling in the silky feel of her skin. He grasped her buttocks and settled her so that she could have no doubt about her effect on him.

Chloe froze.

She hadn't changed her mind, had she? Zach coaxed her closer, sliding his hands up her rib cage to rest under her breasts.

"Zachary? What do I do now?" she asked, her voice quivery.

"Now you go too far, right where you wanted to go, remember?" he said, moving his hands onto her breasts. He rubbed his thumbs over her nipples, already hard little berries. Zach raised his head and used his mouth to nuzzle and suck, until Chloe was gasping for breath.

"I can do that. I know what comes next," she said. Rising, she settled astride him.

Zach put his hands on her hips and guided her onto him. "That's right, sweetheart. This is definitely what comes next." He felt her tense as he entered her feminine sheath. "Relax, baby. I won't hurt you. I swear I will never hurt you."

"I know that. You're too gentle and sweet to ever—" She gasped. "Oh, my. This feels... Oh, Zachary."

He thrust his hips up. "This feels...?"

"Good. Better than good. Fantastic. We fit together, Zachary. For a minute there, I didn't think this was going to work. But we fit."

"We fit perfectly. No one else could ever fit me as well as you do."

"No. No one else but you." Chloe relaxed. Zachary had said exactly the right thing. They were perfect together.

But only temporarily. Nothing that felt this good could last forever. For the first time, though, Chloe could see how a person might be seduced into believing it might last longer than a night, or a week, or a month.

"Ride me, sweetheart, ride me fast and hard."

Chloe smiled indulgently. Zachary chose the most interesting times to assert himself. "I think not. Slow and easy is what I had in mind." She demonstrated. "How does that feel?"

"Slow and easy could work."

"I thought so."

"But not for long. I won't last." Zach surged up and Chloe found herself on her back.

"Okay, hard and fast," she gasped, wrapping her arms around his neck and holding on tight. "You win."

"Trust me, Chloe, no one is going to lose."

After a few moments Chloe had to agree. She'd never felt more like a winner.

Zachary woke as the first sunbeam toyed with the edges of the drawn curtains. Chloe curled next to him, her head nestled trustingly on his shoulder, one hand loosely fisted on his chest.

He felt awful.

As though he'd kicked a puppy or pulled a kitten's tail.

He, Zachary Steele, defender of truth and lover of justice, had taken advantage of a woman's belief in him. Her misplaced belief. He was a cad, a scoundrel, a son of a—

Zach flung one arm over his eyes. Once Chloe found out who and what he was, she would never forgive him. After thirty-one years, he'd finally found the woman he'd been waiting for, and what had he done? He'd *pretended* to be the kind of man she wanted. Nonthreatening. Diffident. Truthful.

He groaned out loud.

Chloe stirred. Adding cowardice to his faults, Zach snapped his eyes shut and feigned sleep. He couldn't face her.

Not yet.

9

Chloe came wide-awake in an instant, not like her usual slow, reluctant journey from oblivion to consciousness. Zachary was sprawled next to her, his arm across her waist and his head on the pillow next to hers. He looked content. Satiated. Thoroughly seduced.

"What have I done?" she whispered, appalled.

She didn't want a temporary lover.

She didn't want a gigolo.

She wanted a husband.

She wanted to be Mrs. Zachary Steele.

She'd fallen in love with him.

Chloe slipped out of the bed. Grabbing the top to his pajamas, she headed for the bathroom. Under the spray of the shower, she tried to settle down and come to terms with her feelings. She did not succeed. Her thoughts and emotions tumbled around inside her head and her heart like lottery numbers in a spinning drum.

She finished her shower and returned to the cabin. Zach hadn't moved. She dressed quickly, in a pair of yellow cotton trousers and a matching sweater.

She sat on the chair beside the bed to lace up her sneakers. When she looked up, she found herself staring into Zachary's dark brown eyes. He didn't look content any longer. He looked... embarrassed. Guilty. As though he thought they'd done something wrong. Chloe's heart sank.

"Good morning," she ventured.

"Is it?" His voice was gruff, making him sound like a surly bear.

"It's early, but it's definitely morning. Good is a matter of opinion, I guess." She stood and fumbled with the doorknob. She had to get away from Zachary's accusing gaze. "I'm going to get coffee. Want me to bring you a cup?" The cheeriness she forced into her voice sounded phony. She never had been a cheerful morning person, even on days when her heart hadn't been breaking.

"Thanks, no. I'll join you as soon as I've showered and shaved."

"Fine. See you later."

She fled the cabin. Why was he being so damn polite? And distant? Had he already forgotten the things they'd done to each other last night?

He hadn't been so polite then. *Hard and fast,* he'd demanded. She'd like to hit him on the chin hard, and then do it again fast.

Chloe opened the doors to the salon. Still fuming, she stalked around the room, looking for something to break. With a shuddering sigh, she forced herself to calm down. As an alternative to other more painful emotions, anger had its advantages, but she couldn't think clearly with mayhem on her mind. Looking around the salon, she spotted a silver coffee urn on the buffet table, along with a basket of croissants and sweet rolls.

Pouring herself a cup of coffee, Chloe continued her survey of the room. She needed a time-out, with something to distract her until she regained control of her disorderly emotions. A bookcase beneath the windows caught her eye. There were several picture albums there. She pulled one out at random and sat on the banquette.

Scanning the photos, she realized the pictures had to be of the Coxes' Florida home. It was very impressive. The photos were not amateur snapshots. They looked like a layout for *Southern Living* or *Architectural Digest*. There were exterior and interior shots, carefully lit and focused.

As she flipped through the pages, pausing now and again when something caught her eye, she couldn't keep her rebellious mind off Zachary. What should she do about him? Confess that she wanted more than a brief affair? Tell him that she'd fallen in love with him?

Heart-stopping terror numbed her.

What if he laughed at her? Worse, what if he pitied her? She had to risk it. She had to be honest with him. Honesty had to be the basis of any relationship, especially one meant to last forever. Chloe ordered her heart to start beating again—it wasn't broken yet, so it might as well get on with its business.

She'd do it. She'd tell him she loved—

Chloe looked at the album page she'd just turned. That little statue on the table—hadn't Dad had one just like it? She looked again. Yes. It was exactly the same. Of course, Mr. Cox had said that he collected pre-Columbian art. But that piece had been returned to...Peru. She was positive. Chloe had gotten very familiar with each object in her father's collection when she and her mother had been trying to discover which countries the pieces had come from.

Chloe turned back to the beginning of the album and went through it again slowly, page by page. She found at least a dozen other photos of pre-Columbian art objects that had once belonged to her father. What could that mean?

She heard footsteps on the deck outside the salon. Quickly she returned the album to its place. She was standing by the buffet, pouring herself another cup of coffee when Zachary came in.

"Zachary, we have to talk. I found something—"

Gerald Cox appeared at the door, accompanied by his wife. "Ah, early risers, I see. Breakfast will be served in a few minutes, as soon as the Arceneauxs join us," their host advised them.

"Does the coffee live up to your high standards, Chloe?" Marian asked, joining her on the banquette.

"Yes, it's very good." Chloe hid her consternation by taking another sip of coffee.

"I'm glad you think so. It's Betancourt's New Orleans blend, my dear," said Gerald. "We're serving Betancourt coffees all day today. Creole coffees tomorrow. Must do this fairly, you know. The captain tells me that the fog has lifted, so we should reach Oak Alley around noon, as we'd planned. Plenty of time for a leisurely tour of the house and grounds after lunch. Later this afternoon, we'll up anchor and set sail for Baton Rouge."

"Great," said Chloe, her mind abuzz with what she'd discovered. She ought to ask Gerald Cox how he'd gotten hold of the items from her father's collection, but something told her to keep quiet until she'd had time to think about it. She'd ask Zachary's advice, too. Maybe there had been something about pre-Columbian art in those art history classes he'd taken. For all she knew, there were multiple copies of every piece that had been in her father's collection. Still, it would be quite a coincidence for the two men to end up with identical collections.

"I'm sure Chloe has seen the river plantations many times, haven't you, my dear?" asked Gerald.

"I've seen Oak Alley before, and a few others, but not in a long time."

Mrs. Cox turned to Zachary, who was standing next to the buffet table. "Have you visited the antebellum mansions before, Zachary?"

"No. I haven't been in Louisiana very long."

"Long enough to charm one of our Southern belles," mused Mrs. Cox.

Gerald handed Zachary a cup of coffee. "Have you two decided on a wedding date yet?"

"No." Zachary's answer was curt and to the point. Chloe's heart thudded painfully. He didn't sound like a man who wanted to make their pretend engagement real. He didn't sound like a man who wanted a temporary affair, either.

Too bad. She wasn't about to settle for a one-night stand. Lifting her chin, Chloe said, "As it turns out, another wedding in the family will take precedence. My mother surprised us by announcing her own engagement recently. She's getting married on Christmas Day."

"Really? I thought she was touring Europe," said Mr. Cox.

"Yes, she is. She met her husband-to-be on the tour."

"How romantic," said Mrs. Cox.

"Here are our missing guests," boomed their host as Emile and Bette Arcenaux entered the room. He rang the ship's bell, and the steward and chef entered, carrying steaming platters of bacon, eggs and biscuits. After arranging the food on the buffet, they withdrew.

"Breakfast is served. Eat hearty," said Mr. Cox.

Chloe finally got a chance to get Zach alone during the tour of Oak Alley. As the rest of the party lingered on the upstairs gallery, admiring the double row of old oaks stretching to the river, she pulled him down the stairs.

"Where are you dragging me?" asked Zachary. He sounded annoyed.

"I have to talk to you. I found—"

He pulled his arm free. "We'll talk later. This is not the time for a morning-after discussion."

Hands fisted on her hips, Chloe glared at him.

"You're acting like an outraged maiden again. I wish you wouldn't do that."

"I may be outraged, but I'm no maiden." Zachary glowered at her.

"No, you're not. But you choose the strangest times to become...assertive. Try to be agreeable while I—"

"Agreeable. Yeah. I'll work on that." He walked away from her.

Chloe hurried after him, following him outside. "Zachary, wait. We have to talk."

"I do not want to talk about last night," he growled. "Not now."

"Oh, good grief. Forget about last night. I found—"

His eyebrows shot up. "Forget about last night? You expect me to forget that you seduced me?"

"All right, don't forget about it. I certainly won't. But, Zachary, something strange is going on."

"Tell me about it." He began walking briskly down the alley of oak trees.

"I'm trying to." She had to almost run to keep up with him. "This morning, when I was alone in the salon, I found something odd. Remember at the reception when Cox told us about his art collection?"

Zachary stopped in his tracks. "I remember. What about it?"

"I found—"

"Ah, there you are. Wait for us, you two," called Marian from the porch of the mansion. "We're heading back to the yacht."

"Pictures of pre-Columbian artifacts."

"Wait. The others are almost here." As the Coxes and Arcenauxs strolled past, Zachary held Chloe's arm, keeping her from following the rest of the party.

"Tell me about it," he ordered, his gaze fixed on her.

Chloe gave him a puzzled glance. She'd seen that look before. The night Zachary had intimidated the Arcenaux cousins. "There's a photo album in the salon, pictures of the Coxes' home and art collection. I found photographs of fifteen pre-Columbian artifacts that I swear belonged to my father."

Zachary's grip on her arm tightened. "Listen to me, Chloe. Don't say one word about this to Cox or anyone else. It could be dangerous."

"Why? Do you think he stole them? How could that be? They were sent back to at least five different countries. I got letters—"

"We'll talk about this later. Now we have to catch up with Cox and the others."

Chloe dug in her heels. "He must have stolen them. No, how could he? But...Sylvie. Zachary, she could have done it. We gave all the pieces to her, along with their histories, and the addresses of the museums to return them to. She must have sold them to Gerald Cox instead."

"Yeah. That's how I figure it, too. Come on, Chloe. They're waiting for us."

"I don't want to go with them. I want to go back to New Orleans today. I have to talk to Sylvie." She paused and stared at him. Zachary was behaving very strangely. "What do you mean, that's how you figure it? Why would any of this concern you?"

"I'll explain everything. Later. Listen to me, Chloe. You will not talk to her. You will not see her. I'll take care of the Sheridan woman."

"You? Why? How? You don't even know her that well."

"I know she's a criminal."

"A criminal? I suppose she is. But she's been my friend for years. Maybe there were extenuating circumstances. I have to give her a chance to explain."

"*No.*" He gave her a shake. "Pay attention. This is important. Forget you saw that album. I'll check it out later. Trust me, Chloe. I will take care of everything."

"You will not. It's my father's collection we're talking about. It has nothing to do with you. But you're right about one thing. I have to go on with the cruise. I need that album. I'll sneak it into my luggage, then I'll confront Sylvie with the pictures."

"You can't do that. We don't have a warr— I mean, taking the album would be stealing. Stealing is against the law."

"I'll give it back when I'm through with it. But I'm sure Mr. Cox is involved in whatever is going on. He's got my father's collection."

"He could be an innocent purchaser." Zach didn't believe that for a minute. Cox had cut short his first visit to New Orleans. He'd left town the day Chloe learned her shipment from Colombia was delayed, and he'd conveniently returned shortly after the shipment had finally arrived. But Chloe hadn't made the connection between her coffee shipments and pre-Columbian artifacts, and he wasn't about to tell her. The less she knew, the safer she would be.

"I don't think so. He has to know Sylvie. Why hasn't he mentioned her to me? He certainly told me about everyone else he knew in New Orleans, when we were discussing mutual acquaintances."

"If he's a crook, why did he leave the album lying around where anyone could see it?"

"Oh. I hadn't thought about that."

"Well, think about it. And keep your mouth shut until we're out of Cox's company. We can't let him know he's under suspicion."

"Suspicion of what? What exactly is going on? And why are you so interested?"

"No time to explain. Here comes Emile. Do as I say, Chloe. Act as if nothing has changed."

"I will not. Everything has changed. You've changed. You're awfully bossy all of a sudden."

"Get used to it, little tyrant. It's about time this relationship got a dose of equality."

"What relationship? We don't have a relationship. This morning you acted as if you never wanted to see me again."

"We're lovers now. And that gives me certain rights and responsibilities."

"Says who? Who made that rule?"

"I did. Cox is coming our way. Shut up and follow my lead."

"What's gotten into you, Zachary? I don't know you anymore."

"You know me. I'm the man who's perfect for you." He winced at the hint of desperation in his voice. Chloe wouldn't hesitate to take over again if he showed the slightest sign of weakness.

"What's this? A lovers' quarrel?" Emile smirked as he drew near.

"Yes," said Chloe.

"No," Zach said, gritting his teeth. He took Chloe by the arm and marched her back to the ship.

Chloe spent the afternoon sitting in a deck chair, pretending to read Mark Twain's *Life on the Mississippi*. Zach knew she wasn't really reading, because the book was upside down in her hands. He wanted to take her to their cabin and make love to her again. And again. As many times as it took to make her look at him the way she had the night before. Now she refused to look at him at all.

He had the definite feeling she wasn't going to let him touch her anytime soon. Which was just as well. He needed to bring the investigation to a successful close before he could tell her everything. Once she knew all the reasons why her company had come under investigation, she'd forgive him.

She had to forgive him.

Between keeping an eye on Chloe and making sure no one moved the album, Zachary kept busy until dinner was served in the salon. The album sat undisturbed on the bottom shelf of the bookcase.

After dinner, Chloe excused herself. "I think I'll go to bed. I feel like I'm coming down with a cold."

"Oh, you poor thing. Would you like some aspirin? Hot tea?"

"No, thank you, Marian. Maybe I'm just tired. I'm sure I'll be fine after a good night's rest."

"Hear that, Steele? The old I've-got-a-headache trick. I knew it. You two are having a fight."

"No, Mr. Arcenaux," Zach said between clenched teeth. "You are wrong. We are not having a fight."

Chloe fled the salon. Zach's instincts told him to follow her, but he had to get the album first.

When he finally returned to the cabin, Chloe appeared to be sleeping. She was wearing his pajama top. Maybe he was grasping at straws, but he had to take that as a good sign. At least she didn't hate his clothing.

He slammed the door shut, and hit the light switch.

Chloe sat up in bed, rubbing her eyes.

"Who is it?"

"Me. Who were you expecting? One of your other temporary lovers?"

"There's no need for sarcasm."

"Sorry. I had to wait hours for Emile and Cox to decide it was time for bed. They were talking about coffee."

"Why did you wait? Why didn't you just leave? Afraid of the reception I'd give you?"

"No. I needed to get hold of the album." He held it up.

"Why?"

"I want you to show me the pieces that were in your father's collection."

"Why?"

"Because. Just do it."

"I don't feel like doing it. Not tonight. Put the album in my suitcase and I'll take it to the museum curator at N.O.M.A. He can verify the items that were supposed to be returned to South America."

"So can I." Zachary sat on the bed and opened it. "Show me."

Chloe snatched the album out of his hands. "Oh, all right." She turned the pages until she found the first item. She pointed. "There. That one came from Peru."

Zach pulled a minicassette recorder out of his jacket pocket and began dictation. "Betancourt Investigation. Affidavit for search warrant. Premises to be searched. Residence of Gerald Cox, St. Petersburg, Florida, address—"

"Stop!"

"Not now, Chloe. I will explain later, I promise. For now, you'll have to trust me. We've got to get through the album so I can get it back to the salon before anyone misses it."

"What Betancourt investigation? Why am I being investigated? Who is investigating me? Why should I trust you? Who are you?"

"I'm one of the good guys."

She didn't look as if she believed that for a minute. "And you think I'm one of the bad guys?" Chloe crossed her arms over her chest and refused to look at him. "I'm not saying another word. Not until you give me the explanation you've been promising all day."

Zach gave up. Exigent circumstances allowed him to reveal his role. And by the stubborn tilt of Chloe's chin, these circumstances were as exigent as they got. "All right. Here it is. I'm a special agent with the U.S. Customs bureau. I've been working undercover as your secretary because someone was using Betancourt's coffee shipments to smuggle pre-Columbian artifacts from a site next to Finca Velásquez. Now it's clear that someone isn't you, but Sylvie Sheridan."

"*Now* it's clear? When did it become clear? Before or after you...we...I..."

"You made love with me? Before. Now, show me the next piece."

He glanced sideways to see how Chloe had taken the revelation, saying a silent prayer that she would not weep. He should have known better. She wasn't crying. She looked ready to explode. "Chloe?"

"Do you have any identification?" She was using her no-nonsense C.E.O. tone with him.

"Not with me."

"Well, then, I'm not sure I believe you." She glared at him through narrowed eyes. "Don't secret agents have rules to follow? You aren't supposed to get...involved with criminals, are you?"

"I'm not a secret agent," Zach said, exasperated. "I'm a special agent, working undercover. And that pretty much requires me to get involved with criminals."

"I don't think you're so special," she sneered. "You shouldn't have let me..." Chloe's eyes widened. "You shouldn't have gone that far, should you? That's why you looked so guilty this morning. You've got that same look on your face right now."

"You're right. I should have told you the truth before we made love. I tried to, but you were all over me and I—"

"Oh! Oh!" Chloe slapped the bed with her hands. "Just like a man. Blame it all on me."

"You're hard to resist, sweetheart," he said soothingly.

Chloe was not placated. "Don't sweetheart me, you low-down, no-good sneaky agent, you!"

"Undercover agent. We don't have time to argue about last night now. Show me the next piece." Zach pointed to the album.

"Oh, all right. Anything to get this fiasco over with." Chloe picked up the album and opened it. She identified each item she'd recognized, but her descriptions were bracketed by grumbled complaints and muttered threats.

Zach ignored her scathing comments on his character and his job as best he could and dictated descriptions and locations of the stolen artwork. When they finished the album, he turned off the recorder. "That should do it. With the information, and what we've learned about Sylvie, we shouldn't have any problem getting warrants to search Cox's home and Sylvie's gallery."

"Why would you search Sylvie's place? All the

items from Dad's collection are accounted for. Cox has them."

"You're forgetting the items smuggled in from Colombia. Sylvie hasn't sold them yet, as far as we know. Cox is probably the buyer."

"That would explain why he canceled the tour of the offices when the shipment from Colombia was delayed. Sylvie must have told him."

"Yeah. Why don't you try to get some sleep? We'll have to play our parts for a few more hours in the morning."

"I'm not sleepy. Zachary, Sylvie must have drugged the coffee that night you and Joe—" She stopped.

But not before he'd seen the concern in her eyes. He relaxed a little. She must care if the memory of the night at the warehouse softened her attitude toward him. "Sylvie does have a key to the warehouse."

She frowned. "I gave it to her. Does that make me an accomplice?"

"No, sweetheart. You're in the clear."

"I'd have been in the clear sooner if you hadn't drunk that coffee, wouldn't I?"

Zach winced. Maybe he'd misread her. Maybe she'd been exhibiting disgust, not sympathy. "Yes. I screwed up that night."

"You're not a very good secret agent, are you? That's not the only night you screwed up. Last night—"

He pounced on her, covering her mouth with his

hand. "That's enough, Chloe. Don't say one more word about last night. Last night was the best night of my life."

She mumbled something against his hand. He removed it. "Because of the sex, I suppose. It should have been good for you. I did all the work." She glared at him.

"It wasn't work, it was fun, and you know it. Come on, sweetheart, don't be mad at me. I couldn't tell you what was going on."

"Zachary...that's not your name, is it? Oh, no! I made love to you, and I don't even know your name."

"My name is Zachary Steele. But everyone but you calls me Zach."

"You used your real name? What kind of secret agent uses his real name? How do I know you're telling me the truth now? Maybe you're the smuggler."

"I am not the smuggler. And I used my real name because this investigation didn't require deep cover, only close surveillance."

"Close surveillance? Oh, I see. That's why you said we were engaged. You thought that would keep us together more. And you were right." Her chin trembled.

"Don't cry, Chloe. Please—"

"Cry? Me? Over you? Fat chance. I'm just a little upset, that's all. A lot upset. Mostly with myself. I certainly made things easy for you, didn't I? I even came up with lagniappe—I bet most agents don't get to sleep with their criminals, do they?"

"No, but then most bosses these days don't get to sleep with their secretaries, either."

"Don't you dare imply that I sexually harassed you. Harassment is unwanted sexual attention. You wanted me."

"And you wanted me. So what is the problem?"

"You lied to me. And I believed every word. What a fool I was."

"You're not a fool, Chloe. You're a warm, trusting woman. And I had to lie. It's my job."

"Some job. That scar on your thigh—it's a bullet wound, isn't it?"

"Yeah," he agreed. "It still gives me trouble now and again." He didn't bother with a stiff upper lip. He let her see his pain. If he could make her feel sorry for him, maybe she'd forgive him sooner.

"Too bad it wasn't a little to the left—then last night wouldn't have happened."

Zach winced. "Chloe! You don't mean that."

"Oh, yes, I do. I'll cooperate with you until this is over because it's my duty as a good, honest, law-abiding citizen. And because I want my company in the clear. But after it's over, I never want to see you again!"

10

"Midnight mass was nice, wasn't it?" asked Claudia Betancourt, sliding her arm around her daughter's waist. The two of them stood side by side looking at the lights on the Christmas tree.

"Yes," agreed Chloe. She couldn't stop looking at the tree, even though it brought back painful memories. One by one, she identified each ornament Zachary had placed on the tree. They'd talked about family and tradition on that wonderful afternoon. And now it was Christmas Eve, and she would never see him again. She sighed.

Her mother squeezed her waist. "Are you sure you're all right, dear?"

"I'm fine, Mother. I'm only sorry my weird moods have messed up your homecoming."

"You haven't messed up anything. The house is perfect, all the wedding arrangements are complete, and you adore John as much as I do. I couldn't ask for anything more."

"I'm glad. It's wonderful to see you so happy."

"I wish you were happy, too. But you have every reason to be 'moody,' as you put it. You've had quite a month, haven't you? I still can't believe Sylvie Sheridan sold your father's collection to that Cox fellow. How could she betray us like that?" Claudia shook her head in disbelief. "After all we did for her, letting her handle your father's collection. There were other galleries we could have used."

Chloe smiled grimly. "Well, she's behind bars now. When they searched her gallery, they found twenty-five artifacts smuggled from Colombia. And some forged paintings, as well."

"Too bad about Mr. Cox. You worked very hard to get that contract with his coffee shops, didn't you?"

"Yes, but I don't think Mr. Cox will be opening any more Coffee Emporiums soon. He'll need all his money for lawyers and bail bondsmen. He's only managed to stay out of jail this long because he's claiming he didn't know the items were stolen."

Claudia smiled. "So much excitement—smugglers and secret agents!"

"Undercover. He was a special agent working undercover. I think secret agents are spies or something." Chloe sighed again. "He was spying on me, so I guess the term fits."

"He seems like a nice young man. At least, he's very polite on the phone, and the messages on the flowers he sends would break your heart. Are you sure you don't want to read them?"

"Yes." She'd already read them, late at night when no one was around to see her getting misty-eyed over a few pretty words. More lies, more than likely.

"All right." Frowning, Claudia reached out to straighten an angel that had gotten turned sideways on the branch where it hung. "He must have finally given up, don't you think? No phone calls or flowers for the last day or two."

"Three."

"Excuse me?"

"It's been three days since he called or sent flowers." Chloe knew to the second the last time she'd heard his voice on the extension telephone. "He must have gone home for Christmas."

"Oh, you're probably right. He'll be back, though."

"Why do you say that? He works in Washington, D.C."

"Not anymore. Didn't you see the ad in the *Times-Picayune* yesterday?"

"Ad? What ad?"

"For the Steele Security Consultant Firm. He must have quit the—what agency did he work for?"

"Customs. He's going to be in New Orleans forever?" Chloe's heart felt as if someone had pinched it. Hard.

"I don't know about forever. But he's bound to be around for some time, since he's opened a business here. The ad said his specialty was providing security to art galleries, museums, and antique dealers. He must know quite a lot about art."

"He does. He writes books about it." The agent who'd come to remove the electronic bugs from her office had told her that. "When he's not sneaking around eavesdropping on people, that is."

"That wasn't very nice, was it? Imagine having your office bugged by your very own government."

"They had a warrant."

"I guess that makes it all right," said Claudia.

"Legal, maybe. But not all right. He heard me, Mother. Zachary overheard me tell Sylvie the kind of man I wanted. Then he turned himself into that man. That was low, and underhanded, and...sneaky."

"Yes, dear. What kind of man do you want?"

"None. I've learned my lesson. You can't trust any of them."

"Oh, no, Chloe. There are many trustworthy men. You can't give up because of one bad experience."

"Two. There was father."

"Oh, Chloe. Your father was not a villain. He wasn't a saint, either. He was just a man."

"A bossy man."

"Being in control was important to him. I let him think he was—it didn't matter to me. Then. I think it might now. But the question won't arise. John and I are going to be partners. I like that. I've gotten stronger—thanks in large part to you, dear. I know I can handle a strong man as an equal. So could you, dear. If you wanted to. You're much more like your father than me, you know."

"That's what Zachary said."

"Perceptive, too. Are you sure he's not the right man for you?"

"It doesn't matter. I don't need a man. I can take care of myself."

"I know you can. But it's natural for a man to want to protect his woman. You could do the same for him, you know. Women do a very good job of taking care of their men. We always have. We don't get the credit because, face it, cooking up a woolly mammoth roast isn't nearly as dramatic as killing the ferocious beast."

"Men don't have to kill our food anymore."

"That must make them worry that we don't need them, don't you think? Zachary, for one, must be convinced by now that you don't need him. Or want him, for that matter."

"What are you saying? That I should give Zachary another chance?"

"You are in love with him, aren't you?"

"I don't know who he is. How could I be in love with him?" Chloe quipped.

"Maybe you only thought you knew the kind of man you wanted. If your heart tells you he's the one…"

"He can't be. He's not…agreeable at all. Mother, he has definite bossy tendencies."

"And you don't?"

"Well, yes."

"That should make for lots of fireworks. You always liked fireworks."

"That was before I found out they can hurt. Don't you think it's time we went to bed? Tomorrow is your wedding day."

"I know. I'm too excited to sleep, but I suppose I should give it a try. I wouldn't want to look like a hag."

"You'll never look like a hag, Mother. But you might have circles under your eyes if you don't get some rest."

"I'll go to bed right now." Claudia started up the stairs.

Chloe followed. "Oh, Mother, I almost forgot. John told me to tell you something when he left to take the others to the hotel—you were talking to Aunt Lou. He said he'd hired the Santa Claus. What's that about?"

"I had a brainstorm, a brilliant brainstorm. I bought the most interesting gifts for everyone in Europe, but if we open gifts before the wedding, the house will be a mess. So, we will leave the gifts unopened until after the ceremony, and then, during the reception, we'll have a Santa Claus hand them out. The guests are all family, after all."

"Oh. Well...that could work."

"Of course it will work. John said he would find one of his students to play the part. College students always need money."

"I guess he succeeded, then." Chloe grinned at her mother as they reached the top of the stairs. "What a good idea. Every Christmas wedding should have a Santa Claus present. That will make the day perfect."

Chloe found herself being fiercely hugged. "I hope so, dear. Oh, I hope so."

* * *

Chloe thought her mother was the most beautiful bride she'd ever seen. The Victorian lace wedding dress she'd chosen suited both the bride and the surroundings. The wedding had gone off without a hitch, and a wonderful Christmas buffet had been eaten and enjoyed by all. Now the guests clustered around the Christmas tree, waiting for Santa.

The doorbell rang.

"I'll get that," said Claudia, handing her champagne flute to her new husband. She hurried into the hallway, returning a few minutes later with a man in a red velvet suit. He was nicely padded, and wore a realistic full white beard.

Chloe smiled widely at her mother, who suddenly appeared nervous. "Too late for bridal jitters, Mother," she murmured.

Claudia led the Santa to the tree, loaded down with presents. Chloe used the distraction to slip from the room and check with the caterer. When she returned, most of the gifts had been distributed, and the guests were busily tearing off bows and wrapping paper. The Santa approached her, a small package in his hand. Chloe frowned. Who could that be from? She and her mother and John had exchanged gifts on Christmas Eve, before going to church.

He was standing in front of her now. She lifted her gaze from the package in his hand to his face. Those eyes! Dark brown, the color of roasted coffee—no, it couldn't be.

Santa handed her the package. She slowly removed the paper and opened the small, square box. A diamond solitaire winked up at her. It looked like an engagement ring.

Before she could ask who the gift was from, Santa went down on one knee in front of her. Chloe was vaguely aware that the room had grown silent, so silent that everyone must be holding their breath. She knew she'd stopped breathing.

"Chloe, I love you. Will you marry me?"

Gasping for air, Chloe tugged down the Santa's beard. It *was* Zachary. "You...you secret agent Santa! You tricked me again. How could you? How could you ruin my mother's wedding, and use Santa Claus to do it?"

He stood. "Your mother hired me. Are you going to answer the question or not?"

Chloe tilted up her chin. "No. I will not marry you. Go away." She handed him the ring box. He took it and shoved it into his pocket.

"You love me. Why won't you marry me?"

"Because you lied to me."

"You used me. For your boy toy."

Chloe gasped. "I did not!"

"Oh, yes, you did. You wanted me to be your gigolo. I forgave you that. Why can't you forgive me?"

"I guess I'm not as agreeable as you are," she sneered.

Zach's bushy white eyebrows snapped together. "That does it. I'll show you agreeable, Chloe. No more Mr. Sweet Guy." Zachary tossed her over his shoulder and carried her out of the room.

"Goodbye, dear," said her mother, waving. "I'll call you when we get back from our honeymoon."

"Mother! Call the police. He's kidnapping me!"

"He is the police, dear. Or was. Have a good time."

Zachary hauled her to a waiting limousine. He stuffed her into the back seat, following closely behind her. The driver immediately pulled away from the curb.

"Are you stealing someone's limo?"

"Nope. I hired this one. I thought it might bring back pleasant memories of another limousine ride we shared."

"I don't have any pleasant memories where you're concerned."

"You're a lousy liar, Chloe."

"I'm not a professional, like you."

"I did not lie to you about anything important."

"Oh, no? Who you are isn't important? Where you're from? Who your family is? What you do for a living?"

"My name is Zachary Steele. I'm from Elizabeth City, North Carolina, and my father runs a charter ship business and my mother teaches school. Just as I told you."

"And your sister?"

He got that guilty look on his face. "I don't have a sister."

"Aha! See, you lied."

"So I lied. Big deal. Are you going to marry me or not?"

"I already answered that question. Take me home."

"Not until you look me in the eye and tell me you don't love me."

She looked out the window instead. "You look ridiculous in that Santa suit."

"It was the only way I could think of to get close to you."

"Close surveillance is your specialty, isn't it?"

"Do you love me, Chloe?" He put a finger on her chin and gently turned her around to face him.

"All right, you win. I love you." She spat the words at him. "But I'm not going to marry you. I could never marry a man who lies." She paused, and took a deep, shuddering breath. "But I suppose we could have an affair."

"Fine." Zachary brushed a kiss on her mouth. "We'll have an affair."

Outraged, she pushed him away. "What do you mean, fine? You'd settle for an affair? After all we've been through together? Don't you want to marry me?"

"I asked you, didn't I?" He took the velvet box from his pocket. "Remember this? Me, on my knees?"

"Of course, I remember. It was only a few minutes ago that you proposed. You changed your mind awfully fast." She reached for the box.

He jerked it back. "Not so fast. You turned me down."

"What did you expect? I told you from the beginning I wasn't interested in marriage. I never lied to you."

"Okay, you don't want to get married. I'm willing to compromise. I realize a relationship should be a no-one-is-boss kind of thing—a partnership, not a dictatorship. Your mother and I discussed that at length—not easy, since you were listening in most of the time. A very wise woman, your mother. She's a great believer in compromise, so—"

Chloe grabbed him by his ermine collar. "Listen to me, Zachary Steele. You're not getting anywhere near me until I have a wedding ring to go with that flashy engagement ring you almost gave me. We're getting married and that's all there is to it!"

He raised his fake white eyebrows. "Does that mean you lied about wanting an affair?"

"I did not lie. I changed my mind. That is a woman's prerogative, after all. I don't want an affair. I want to get married." She shook him.

"Okay. Whatever you say, sweetheart."

She eyed him suspiciously. "You gave in awfully easy."

"I've always been easy where you're concerned. And sweet. I'll always be sweet to you, Chloe. I promise."

"All right. But not too sweet. I want sweet and nice and agreeable, but I want stubborn and bossy and arrogant, too. I don't want to give up the fireworks. I've always loved fireworks. Almost as much as I love you."

"Merry Christmas, Chloe." He took the ring out of the box and slipped it on her finger.

Chloe wrapped her arms around his neck. "Merry Christmas, my secret agent Santa."

* * * * * *

Silhouette Books

invites you to celebrate the joys of the season December 1998 with the Fortune Family in...

A FORTUNE'S CHILDREN CHRISTMAS

Three Fortune cousins are given exactly one year to fulfill the family traditions of wealth and power. And in the process these bachelors receive a Christmas gift more precious than mere riches from three very special women.

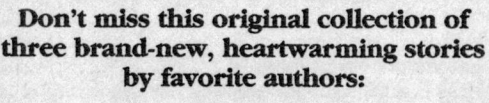

Don't miss this original collection of three brand-new, heartwarming stories by favorite authors:

Lisa Jackson
Barbara Boswell
Linda Turner

Look for **A FORTUNE'S CHILDREN CHRISTMAS** this December at your favorite retail outlet. And watch for more Fortune's Children titles coming to Silhouette Desire, beginning in January 1999.

Look us up on-line at: http://www.romance.net

PSFORTUNE

Take 2 bestselling love stories FREE

Plus get a FREE surprise gift!

Special Limited-Time Offer

Mail to Silhouette Reader Service™

3010 Walden Avenue
P.O. Box 1867
Buffalo, N.Y. 14269-1867

YES! Please send me 2 free Silhouette Yours Truly™ novels and my free surprise gift. Then send me 4 brand-new novels every other month, which I will receive months before they appear in bookstores. Bill me at the low price of $2.90 each plus 25¢ delivery and applicable sales tax, if any.* That's the complete price, and a saving of over 10% off the cover prices—quite a bargain! I understand that accepting the books and gift places me under no obligation ever to buy any books. I can always return a shipment and cancel at any time. Even if I never buy another book from Silhouette, the 2 free books and the surprise gift are mine to keep forever.

201 SEN CH72

Name _____ (PLEASE PRINT)

Address _____ Apt. No. _____

City _____ State _____ Zip _____

This offer is limited to one order per household and not valid to present Silhouette Yours Truly™ subscribers. *Terms and prices are subject to change without notice. Sales tax applicable in N.Y.

USYT-98 ©1996 Harlequin Enterprises Limited

**Coming in December 1998
from Silhouette Books...**

The BIG BAD WOLFE family is back!

WOLFE WINTER

by bestselling author

Joan Hohl

Officer Matilda Wolfe had followed in her family's law-enforcement footsteps. But the tough beauty swore she wouldn't fall in love as easily as the rest of the Wolfe pack.

Not this Christmas, not during this case…
and not with an ex-mercenary turned minister whose sexy grin haunted her dreams.

Don't miss the brand-new single-title release
WOLFE WINTER this December 1998…
only from Silhouette Books.

Available at your favorite retail outlet.

Look us up on-line at: http://www.romance.net

PSWINWOLF

For a limited time, Harlequin and Silhouette have an offer you just can't refuse.

In November and December 1998:

BUY **ANY** TWO HARLEQUIN
OR SILHOUETTE BOOKS and
SAVE $10.00
off future purchases

OR BUY ANY THREE HARLEQUIN OR SILHOUETTE BOOKS
AND **SAVE $20.00** OFF FUTURE PURCHASES!

(each coupon is good for $1.00 off the purchase of two
Harlequin or Silhouette books)

....

JUST BUY 2 HARLEQUIN OR SILHOUETTE BOOKS, SEND US YOUR NAME, ADDRESS AND 2 PROOFS OF PURCHASE (CASH REGISTER RECEIPTS) AND HARLEQUIN WILL SEND YOU A COUPON BOOKLET WORTH **$10.00 OFF** FUTURE PURCHASES OF HARLEQUIN OR SILHOUETTE BOOKS IN 1999. SEND US 3 PROOFS OF PURCHASE AND WE WILL SEND YOU 2 COUPON BOOKLETS WITH A TOTAL **SAVING OF $20.00.** (ALLOW 4-6 WEEKS DELIVERY) OFFER EXPIRES DECEMBER 31, 1998.

....

I accept your offer! Please send me a coupon booklet(s), to:

NAME: _____

ADDRESS: _____

CITY: _____ STATE/PROV.: _____ POSTAL/ZIP CODE: _____

Send your name and address, along with your cash register receipts for proofs of purchase, to:

In the U.S.	In Canada
Harlequin Books	Harlequin Books
P.O. Box 9057	P.O. Box 622
Buffalo, NY	Fort Erie, Ontario
14269	L2A 5X3

PHQ4982

SILHOUETTE YOURS TRULY™

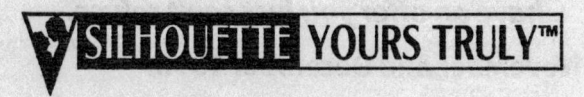

Sneak Previews of January titles from Yours Truly™:

THE LAW AND GINNY MARLOW
by Marie Ferrarella
The Cutlers of the Shady Lady Ranch

All Ginny Marlow wanted to do was bail her little sister out of a small-town jail. But when she got to Serendipity, Montana, the hunky sheriff sentenced *her!* Now she had to spend ten days on Quint Cutler's ranch if she wanted to take her sister home. Faced with good old-fashioned home cooking, warm fires…and seductive sunsets with a certain sexy sheriff, this feisty lawyer was suddenly appealing to the law to turn her ten-day trial into a life sentence of love.

THE MILLIONAIRE AND THE PREGNANT PAUPER
by Christie Ridgway
Follow That Baby

When the New Year arrived, instead of partying hard, oil tycoon Michael Wentworth was smiling softly at a beautiful stranger's newborn. Worse, everyone seemed to think *he* was the proud papa of Beth Masterson's bouncing baby boy. Well…Michael *did* need a temporary wife to gain his inheritance, and the struggling, unwed mom sure could use a man to set up house with—and maybe even a happily ever after. But was marriage-resistant Michael ready to be that man?